P9-BHV-109

THE RUGRATS™ FILES
A TIME TRAVEL ADVENTURE

CASE OF THE MISSING GOLD

by David Lewman

SCHOLASTIC INC.
New York Toronto London Auckland Sydney
Mexico City New Delhi Hong Kong

KLASKY
CSUPO INC.

Based on the TV series *Rugrats*® created by Arlene Klasky, Gabor Csupo, and Paul Germain as seen on Nickelodeon®

ISBN 0-439-23204-X

12 11 10 9 8 7 6 5 4 3 2 1   0 1 2 3 4 5/0

Printed in the U.S.A.

First Scholastic printing, September 2000

CHAPTER 1

Tommy pressed his nose up against the glass bowl and looked at the fish. "What's his name, Chuckie?" he asked.

"Oscar," said Chuckie, grinning. "My dad says he's a goatfish."

Chuckie had brought his new pet over to Tommy's house for his best friend to see. They watched a little goldfish swim slowly around the bowl.

"He doesn't *look* like a goat," said Tommy.

Just then Grandpa Lou came into the living room. "What have you sprouts got there?" he asked. He leaned over and looked in the glass bowl.

"A goldfish, eh?" Grandpa Lou chuckled. "Looks like a little gold nugget swimming around in there. Reminds me of my days hunting for gold. Spike, off my chair, please."

Spike jumped down from the overstuffed

armchair. Grandpa Lou brushed Spike's hairs off the chair and sat down. "Yep," he continued, "I headed west to go prospectin' in the gold country—once found *fifteen* gold nuggets in a single day!"

Tommy and Chuckie toddled over to Grandpa Lou's chair. "I was a forty-niner," Grandpa Lou said. "'Course, that was *nineteen*-forty-nine. The original forty-niners were prospectors way back in *eighteen*-forty-nine. They hunted for gold. You sprouts want to hear about 'em?"

Tommy crawled up to his lap and smiled. Grandpa chuckled. "I guess you do."

But before Grandpa Lou could begin, the doorbell rang. Tommy's dad, Stu, opened the door. Betty stood on the front step with her twins, Phil and Lil. She was wearing a tool belt.

"Hey there, Stu," said Betty. "Didi called for help with a leaky faucet. Where's she hiding?"

"She's in the kitchen, Betty," said Stu. "Come on in."

Betty stepped into the living room. "Hiya, Lou," she said. "Looks like you're havin' a meeting here. Mind if my pups join in?"

"Not at all, Betty," said Grandpa Lou. "We were just talking about huntin' for gold."

"Gold, huh? Well, let me know when you find some," Betty said, chuckling as she headed into the kitchen.

Phil and Lil sat on the floor with Chuckie.

"Well, let's see, where were we?" Grandpa asked. "Oh yeah, it was January of eighteen forty-eight when a man named James Marshall found a few pieces of gold at a sawmill on the American River in California. He showed 'em to his boss, John Sutter, who asked him to keep the gold a secret."

Grandpa Lou winked at the babies, then continued. "Gold was worth a lot of money in those days, just like it is today, and if the secret got out, people would come looking for the gold. If you had gold, you could buy anything you wanted. And even though they didn't have TV or telephones back then, they had newspapers, and word of the gold spread! And the next year, eighteen forty-nine, *thousands* and *thousands* of people came from *all* over the world to hunt for gold in California."

Grandpa Lou stretched his arms above him and yawned.

"And they couldn't fly to California back then, either," Grandpa Lou said. "They had to sail over the ocean or ride on wagons across the prairies and the mountains. It took weeks and weeks, and it sure wasn't easy."

He yawned again. "Once they got to California, people thought they could simply pick the gold right off the ground. They didn't realize they had to pan for it in the river or dig for it in a gold mine. Some of the forty-niners found big nuggets of gold! But most of 'em didn't find anything more than a few flakes. Or a sprinkling of gold dust. Like the . . . dust that's . . . getting in . . . my eyes. . . ."

Grandpa Lou tilted his head back and closed his eyes. Then he began to snore. He had fallen asleep! Tommy climbed down from his lap.

"Hey, Chuckie," Tommy said. "Oscar's not a goatfish. He's a goldfish!"

"Yeah," said Chuckie, smiling. He went back to Oscar's bowl and looked at him fondly. "Your grandpa said he looks like a little gold nugget."

"We get nuggets in Smiley Meals," said Phil.

Lil said, "First we dip them in sticky sauce, then we eat them."

"Nuggets are okay, but I'd rather have this!" Angelica, Tommy's older cousin, had come into the room and heard the twins talking. She was eating a Reptar Bar.

"Angelica," said Lil, licking her lips, "can I have a bite of your Reptar Bar? Please?"

"Sorry," said Angelica, "there's only enough for me." She stuffed the rest of the chocolate into her mouth.

"I wish *we* had Reptar Bars," said Phil.

"Well," said Angelica, swallowing, "alls you got to do is go to the store and give them some monies, and they'll give you Reptar Bars."

"But, Angelica," said Chuckie sadly, "we don't *gots* any monies."

"Then I guess you don't get any Reptar Bars!" she answered, laughing. Reaching into her backpack, Angelica pulled out her doll, Cynthia, and began to brush her hair.

"Hey, I gots an idea," said Tommy. "Grandpa

said gold nuggets are worth lots of monies, right?"

"Right . . ." said Chuckie, Phil, and Lil.

"And if you have gold, you can buy anything you want!"

"Right . . ." said Chuckie, Phil, and Lil.

"So alls we gots to do is find some gold nuggets! Then we'll have monies to buy lots of Reptar Bars!"

Angelica stopped playing. If I had a lot of gold, she thought, I could buy the Cynthia Workout Center and the Cynthia Swimming Pool and the Cynthia Luxury Mansion . . .

"But how are we gonna find gold, Tommy?" asked Chuckie.

Tommy thought. "Well, Grandpa said the shorty-niners had to dig for it. So first we gotta get our digging tools. C'mon, let's go out to the sandbox."

Angelica hopped up and pulled on her backpack. "Wait up, babies," she said. "You need me to help you find gold." And I'll keep it all for myself, she thought.

"Thanks, Angelica!" said Tommy. "That's real nice of you!"

"Of course," Angelica replied with a smirk.

Tommy and his friends went out to the backyard, bringing Spike along with them. "Spike's a good digger," said Tommy. "He can help us find gold."

As they all headed toward the sandbox to get shovels, Tommy's mom, Didi, came out to the backyard with his little brother, Dil. Dil was in a stroller, shaking a rattle. "Mine!" he declared happily.

"Hey, Deedster," Betty called from the kitchen, "where do you keep your monkey wrench?"

"I'm not sure we have a monkey wrench, Betty, but I'll check," said Didi, heading into the house. "I'll be right back, kids."

Tommy picked up a shovel. "All right," he said, "who wants to dig for gold, just like the shorty-niners?"

"Me!" shouted Lil.

"Me!" yelled Phil.

"Me . . . I guess," said Chuckie, a little nervously.

"Mine! Mine!" said Dil.

"Wait just a minute, Tommy Pickles," said

Angelica. "We can't *all* go looking for gold."

Everyone stared at her. "Why not, Angelica?" asked Tommy.

They didn't know that Angelica had a plan—to get as much gold as possible for herself. The fewer people she had to share it with, the better. Angelica quickly made up a reason. "Because one of us has to stay with Dil. I'd say . . . Finster." Angelica pointed at Chuckie. "He'd just get scared, anyway."

"Why can't Dil go?" asked Tommy.

"Because he was just born practically yesterday," explained Angelica, disgusted. "He doesn't know *anything* about finding gold."

"Um, sure he does," said Tommy, trying to think quickly. "Hey, Dilly," he said, "where do you find gold?"

"Mine, mine!" said Dil.

"See," Tommy said proudly. "Dil knows you find gold in a mine, just like Grandpa said."

Angelica was not impressed. "He says that all the time! He thinks everything is his!"

"Reminds me of someone I know," a voice sang out.

10

"Who said that?" demanded Angelica.

"I did," said Susie Carmichael as she pushed up a board in the fence and crawled into Tommy's backyard.

"Hi, Susie!" said Tommy. He was happy to see his neighbor. She was a big kid, and she always helped them stand up to Angelica.

"Hi, Tommy! Whatcha doing?" asked Susie.

"None of your business, Susie," said Angelica.

"We're going to go find some gold so we can get Reptar Bars," said Tommy. "Wanna come?"

"Well," said Susie, thinking about what she'd heard through the fence, "only if Dil and Chuckie come too."

"Would that be all right, Angelica?" asked Chuckie.

Annoyed, Angelica threw her hands up in the air. "Sure, why not? Let's bring everyone in the neighborhood! And while we're at it, let's bring Santa Claus, and the Easter Bunny, and the Tooth Fairy, too!"

"I don't think they live around here," said Lil doubtfully.

"Great!" said Tommy. "Let's go find some gold!"

Everybody except Angelica cheered. Even Spike barked. They picked up shovels, pails, and sippy cups. "Come on, Cynthia," said Angelica to her doll. "It looks like everyone in town is going."

Susie stuck her head back through the fence and told her mom she was going to be in Tommy's backyard for a while. Chuckie peeked through a window and waved to Oscar. "Bye, Oscar! Don't worry, I'll be right back!" he said. Then he hurried back to his friends. "Uh, where are we going, Tommy?" he asked.

"Well," said Tommy, "Grandpa said that man found his gold by a river, right?"

"Yeah," said Phil, nodding.

"So alls we gots to do is find a river!"

"There's one!" shouted Lil, pointing.

Sure enough, there was a trickle of water coming out of the kitchen door, across the patio, and into the grass. The water was actually coming from the leaky faucet inside the house that Didi and Betty were trying to fix, but

Tommy and his friends didn't know that. They ran over to the stream of water and followed it into the bushes.

Tommy led the way. As he pushed through the last bush, he looked up and gasped. "Wow," he said, amazed.

CHAPTER 2

Right in front of Tommy and his friends was a wide, rolling valley with brown hills and green trees. In the middle of the valley stood a tall wooden building with a flag flying from its roof. The building was surrounded by a high wall with towers in each corner.

"What is that?" asked Phil, who had never seen anything like it before.

"I think it's Santa's house," said Lil.

"Where's the snow?" asked Phil.

"Maybe the elves shoveled it up," said Lil.

Tommy started walking toward the building. The others followed him.

"I know what it is," said Susie. "It's a fort."

But Angelica shook her head. "Naah," she said, "if that was a fort, there'd be guards all around it."

"Halt!"

They all froze. An older boy stepped out

from behind a tree. He was dressed in jeans, a loose shirt, and a big floppy hat. "Who goes there?" he asked.

"We go there!" said Tommy in a friendly voice. "My name's Tommy. What's yours?"

"My name is Parker. Why are you going to Fort Sutter?"

"See?" whispered Susie. "I told you it was a fort."

"Nobody likes a know-it-all, Susie," said Angelica.

Tommy was about to answer, when suddenly a huge crowd of people rushed by! They were carrying shovels, pickaxes, and iron pans, and they all seemed to be in a very big hurry. Their boots kicked up clouds of dust as they ran.

Some of them even dropped their tools as they sprinted away. "Hey!" yelled Tommy. "You dropped your—"

"No time to stop!" shouted one of the runners. "Got to get to the mill!"

"Ohhhh," said Phil, "they're running to get milk. I'd like some too."

"'Specially if it's chocolate," said Lil.

"Not milk," corrected Parker, "mill. They're all

going to Sutter's sawmill. Pretty soon there won't be anyone left around here."

"Hmm," said Angelica, "those tools they dropped might be handy for digging." She picked up the pans and pickaxes left in the dirt.

Tommy watched the crowd disappear into the distance. "Why is everybody running to a sawed mill when they could play in a really great fort?" he asked.

"Because they've got gold fever," explained Parker.

"Will they have to get a shot?" asked Lil.

"My mommy's a doctor," said Susie, "and she says if you've got a fever, you shouldn't be running around outside."

"They're not sick," said Parker. "They just think they're going to strike it rich. This fort used to be the biggest thing around here, full of people working and trading. But ever since James Marshall found gold at the sawmill, everybody's run off to go prospecting. I suppose you will too."

"You got it, buster," said Angelica. "We're not going to let everyone else get all the gold." She tried to load some of the mining tools onto Spike's back, but Spike ran off to hide. Angelica passed out the tools, making everybody carry one. She even slipped a pan into Dil's stroller.

Dil grinned happily. "Mine!" he declared.

"I know who those peoples were!" Tommy suddenly cried out. "They were the shorty-niners, just like Grandpa said!"

"Shorty-niners?" said Parker, confused.

"This is great!" said Tommy. "We're in the right spot! Now alls we gots to do is follow those shorty-niners to the mill."

"But after we get to the mill, how do we find the gold?" Lil asked.

"That's easy, Lil," said Tommy. "We just, um, look for it, and um, dig a little bit, and . . . Parker, do you know how to find gold?"

Parker sighed. He wished more people would stay at Fort Sutter instead of running off to the mill. But once people got the idea of gold in their heads, it seemed there was no stopping them. Some people even dug right under the fruit trees around the fort, thinking that gold nuggets might be caught in the roots.

"I can see that you've got a touch of the gold fever yourself," Parker said. "Well, once you reach the mill, you'll see prospectors using their pans and shovels to search for gold along the river. That's how most people do it."

"Okeydokey, Parker!" said Tommy. "Then that's how we'll do it too."

"But," said Parker, lowering his voice, "some people don't bother to pick through the gravel along the river. They hunt for the mother lode."

"Why would they hunt for the mother toad?" asked Chuckie.

"Maybe they want to get warts," said Phil.

"Not mother toad," said Parker impatiently, "Mother *lode*. Look, all those little bits of gold in the river had to come from somewhere, right?"

"I guess so," said Chuckie.

"Maybe the Sandy Man bringed them," said Lil, "and dropped them in the river so the fishies could go to sleep."

"Everybody knows the sandman brings sand, not gold," said Angelica. "Gold must come from the Gold Man."

Chuckie shuddered. "The Gold Man?"

"No!" said Parker. "The little bits of gold came down the river from the mountains. Somewhere in the mountains, buried deep in the rock where the rivers begin, must be a huge mother lode of gold!"

In his imagination Chuckie then saw a gigantic, solid gold mother stomping down the mountains. She threw back her head and roared, like Reptar. Then she started to run, because the Gold Man was chasing her. "Maybe looking for gold isn't such a good idea," Chuckie said, trembling.

Parker stared at Chuckie. "You certainly do have very red hair. It almost looks like your head is burning."

"Yeah, well, it's not," Chuckie said, patting his head. "See? If my head were burning, I couldn't touch it like this."

"One of my best friends told me a story his grandmother knew about a boy with hair like fire," said Parker.

"C'mon, let's go," said Angelica. "We don't gots time to listen to a boring old story."

"It's about finding gold," said Parker.

"Well, maybe we could stay for a minute or two," said Angelica.

Parker leaned against a tree. Everyone else sat on the ground and listened to his tale.

"Long, long ago, when the land was new—" Parker said.

"That's not how you start a story," said Lil. "You're supposed to say, 'Once upon a slime—'"

"No, it's, 'Once upon a dime,'" said Phil.

"No it isn't, Philip."

"Yes it is, Lillian."

"SLIME!"

"DIME!"

Lil pushed Phil onto the ground. He tickled Lil, and she started giggling while they rolled around. Spike ran over and started licking them, making them laugh even more.

"Go ahead, Parker," said Susie. "they're listening to you."

"Anyway," said Parker, "a long time ago, the mountains burned night and day. Instead of snow on top, they had fire, and the fire could run down the mountains, burning everything in its path."

"This story is kinda scary," Chuckie whispered to Tommy.

"It's okay, Chuckie," whispered Tommy, "it's just a story."

Parker continued. "The people went to their leader and said, 'The mountain-fire has burned our trees, our grass, and our homes. You must go to the mountain and ask him to put out his fire.' But the leader was afraid and said, 'I cannot go. I must stay here and lead the tribe.'"

"That leader was a fraidycat," said Phil.

"Maybe he was just being careful," said Chuckie.

"Shh!" said Lil.

Parker went on. "The people said, 'If no one asks the mountain to put out his fire, soon there will be no one to lead.' Just then the leader's small grandson stepped forward and said, 'I will go.'"

"Wow, that was brave!" said Tommy.

"Aw, what's the big deal?" asked Angelica. "It's just a stupid old mountain. It can't chase you or anything."

Parker said, "So the boy went to the biggest

mountain and told him, 'Your fire is burning everything we have. Can you and your mountain brothers please put your fire out?'"

"The mountain said, 'My fire shines bright red, like the sun before it sets. What will you give me if I put out my fire?' And the boy said, 'Something that shines bright yellow, like the sun at noon.' So the mountain said, 'Give it to me, and I will put out my fire.'"

Parker pretended to take something out of his pocket. "So the boy reached into his pocket and pulled out a shiny rock. 'I'll give you this,' he said to the mountain. 'It's the nicest thing I have.'"

"I'll bet it was a magic rock," said Susie. "Right, Parker?"

"Wait and see," he answered. "The mountain liked the shiny rock so much that he decided to trade. He turned his fire into bright red hair, which became the boy's hair. And he hid the shiny rock in a deep, dark hole, where it grew into a giant block of gold."

"The mother lode!" said Tommy.

"That's right," said Parker. "Since that day,

the tops of the mountains have been covered with snow, not fire. Someday the boy with hair red as fire is supposed to return to the mountains and find the hidden gold."

They all turned and looked at Chuckie.

"Don't look at me!" he said. "I'm not going into a deep, dark hole . . . I don't care how much gold is in it!"

"Oh, yes you are, Finster, and the sooner the better!" said Angelica. "C'mon, shorty-niners, we've wasted enough time already. Let's go!"

With that, Angelica jumped up and started running in the direction the crowd of gold hunters had gone. The others all got up to follow her. Susie pushed Dil's stroller, and Spike ran alongside Tommy.

"Bye-bye, Parker," Tommy yelled over his shoulder. "Thanks for telling us about the gold at the mill!"

"Good luck!" called Parker. Then he added softly, "You're going to need it."

CHAPTER 3

The crowd of gold hunters had left a trail that was easy to follow. There were hundreds of boot prints in the dirt, and every few hundred feet or so would be something dropped along the way, like a hat or a handkerchief.

"They sure were in a big hurry," said Chuckie.

"That's because they want to get to the sawmill before all the gold is gone," Angelica said. "C'mon, we gotta go faster!" She sprinted ahead, and the others ran as fast as they could to keep up.

But Lil quickly grew weary and plopped herself down on a rock by the trail. "I gotta rest!" she gasped. "I'm all outta bread!"

"Lil!" cried Phil. He ran back and sat beside Lil. Soon everybody else noticed the twins had fallen behind, so they came back to join them.

"Great," grumbled Angelica, "now all the

bestest gold will be gone."

Spike was sniffing around the rocks and bushes where they sat. He kept sticking his nose into the holes in the ground. There were lots of them.

"These holes are awfully big for worms," said Phil.

"Maybe they're snake holes," said Susie.

"Snakes?" yelled Chuckie, jumping up.

"It's okay, Chuckie," said Susie. "We have a snake in a glass box at my school, and it's very nice. My teacher says most snakes are our friends."

"Maybe *your* friends," said Angelica, "not mine."

Susie ignored Angelica. "My teacher also said there are dangerous snakes. But almost none of them live here."

"Which ones *do* live here, Susie?" asked Chuckie in a shaky voice.

"Well, um, let's see . . . there's coral snakes, and copperheads, and um, rattlesnakes . . ."

Just then they heard a loud rattling sound! Chuckie screamed and tried to climb up on

Angelica's shoulders. Phil held on to Lil. Spike started to bark.

"Nobody move," whispered Susie. "My teacher said that if you ever hear a rattlesnake, you should be real still."

"How can I be still when Finster's trying to stand on my head?" Angelica fumed.

"Shh!" said Tommy.

They all got quiet and stood as still as they could. *Chukah—chukah—chukah*. Everyone held their breath. Then Tommy looked in the stroller. Dil was shaking his rattle!

"Aw, it's just Dil!" said Tommy, relieved.

"Rad-o! Rad-o!" said Dil, shaking his rattle as fast as he could.

"Oh, brother," said Angelica. "Finster, get down!"

They'd been walking for a long time and still hadn't reached the sawmill. Everyone was getting tired.

"How much more do we have to go?" whined Lil.

"How should we know?" snapped Angelica. "We've never been to this sawmill place before."

"What is a sawed mill, anyway?" asked Phil.

"It's where they saw things," explained Susie, "like logs and boards and stuff."

"Will they have juice pops?" Lil asked.

Before anyone could answer, they all heard a very loud rattling.

"Dil's getting really good with that rattle," said Phil, impressed.

"Yeah," agreed Susie, "I've never heard a baby shake a rattle so fast."

"Um, guys," said Chuckie, "Dil's not shaking his rattle."

They looked at Dil. He was fast asleep. Suddenly Susie spotted something and yelled out to Tommy, who was walking ahead. "Tommy, stop!"

Tommy froze. Then he saw it. Right in front of him, in the middle of the path, was a big rattlesnake! Coiled like a thick rope, the snake held up its tail and shook its rattles angrily. It was ready to strike.

"Don't move, Tommy," whispered Susie.

"Okay," whispered Tommy. "I'll be real still."

But the snake kept shaking its rattle and didn't turn its head away. It opened its mouth, and Tommy could see its long fangs.

Spike started to growl.

"Susie, don't let Spike jump at the rattlesnake!" Tommy whispered.

Very slowly Susie put her hand around Spike's collar.

"This is bad," Chuckie moaned, "real bad. What are we going to do?"

Suddenly they heard another rattle! The babies groaned—not another rattlesnake!

"Whatever we do," whispered Phil, "now we gots to do it twice."

The other rattle seemed to confuse the snake. Flicking its pointy tongue, the snake tasted the air, trying to see where the sound was coming from.

"It's Dil!" whispered Tommy. They all took their eyes off the snake for a second to look at Dil. He had awakened and was shaking his toy rattle.

"Dil, stop!" hissed Angelica. "You gotta be quiet!"

But the snake rattled back in answer to Dil. Dil giggled, and shook his rattle harder. The rattlesnake slithered forward, until it lay only a few feet in front of Dil's stroller. Everyone held their breath.

Dil smiled at the snake and shook his rattle again. To everyone's surprise—and relief—the snake bobbed its head once, turned around, and quickly slipped away, disappearing into the underbrush.

"Good for you, Dilly!" shouted Tommy. "You told that snake to go home!"

"Dil can talk to snakes!" exclaimed Phil.

"Do you think he can talk to worms, too?" Lil asked excitedly.

"Okay, okay," said Angelica, "let's get out of here before Dil's playmate comes back!" The adventurers hurried on, finally coming to an unfinished wooden building next to a river.

"That must be the sawmill," Susie said.

"Look at that!" cried Tommy.

"All I see is a house with lots of pieces missing," said Phil.

"No, Phil," said Tommy, "look at all the shorty-niners!"

Phil looked harder. There were people everywhere—at the river, on the hills, by the trees. All of them were digging like crazy, hoping to find gold.

CHAPTER 4

"It looks kinda like the place with all the snake holes," said Phil, "only with bigger holes."

He was right. Everywhere they looked, the ground had been dug up. The holes were so close together, the gold-hunters were shoveling dirt out of one hole and right into another. Some diggers were yelling at each other about where the dirt should go.

Others were standing in the river, swirling wet mud and gravel around in big pans. When there was almost nothing left in the pans, they'd pick through the tiniest bits at the bottom with their fingers. Then they'd look disappointed, sigh, and scoop more dirt into their pans.

"Kinda crowded, isn't it?" said Susie.

"I told you we needed to get here sooner," said Angelica.

"Let's talk to a shorty-niner," said Tommy.

They walked over to a guy using a pan by the river. He stopped spilling water out of the pan when he saw them coming.

"Hi!" said Tommy. "Can you—"

"What do you want?" he asked suspiciously. "This spot's taken. You're not claim-jumpers, are you?"

"No, I don't think so," answered Tommy. "Sometimes we're bed-jumpers."

"What's clam-jumping?" asked Phil. "Sounds kinda fun."

"And smelly," added Lil, clapping her hands.

"Not clam-jumping," said the prospector, "*claim*-jumping. How long you been here in the gold country?"

"We just got here today," said Susie.

"Oh, tenderfeet, huh?" he said. Tommy and his friends looked at their feet, puzzled. "Well, this is my claim," he explained, gesturing toward a small area around him. "I'm the only one who can pan for gold here. Anyone else who tries is a claim-jumper, see?"

Tommy nodded. "How do you pan for gold?"

The prospector rubbed his chin. "Before I

start answering all of your questions, suppose you answer a couple of mine."

"Okay," said Tommy.

"First of all," he said, "which way did you come to Californy? Around the Horn? Across Panama? Or over the Oregon Trail?"

"We crawled through some bushes in my backyard," said Tommy.

The prospector stared at him for a second. "Uh-huh. And what do you plan to do with your gold once you find it?"

"That's easy," said Tommy, smiling. "Buy Reptar Bars."

The prospector stared at Tommy. "All right, fine," he finally said, turning back to his work. "You keep your secrets, and I'll keep mine."

"What secrets?" asked Chuckie. But the man wouldn't talk to them anymore. He just kept scooping gravel and dirt up with his pan, adding water, and sloshing it around.

"Well, thanks, anyway," said Tommy, still friendly. "C'mon, guys, he's real busy right now. Let's talk to another shorty-niner."

"Okay," said Angelica, "I'll do the talking."

Angelica looked around until she spotted a young man next to the river. Smiling her sweetest smile, Angelica walked over with the others. "Hi there, Mr. Shorty-niner Person. My name is Angelica. What's yours?"

Startled, the prospector looked up from his pan. "Sam," he said.

"So, um, whatcha doin', Sam?"

"Panning for gold."

"How much have you found?" Angelica was hoping Sam had found enough pieces of gold that he'd be willing to share some with her.

"None."

"Oh," said Angelica, disappointed. But then she thought that if she couldn't get any gold from Sam, she might as well try to get some information. "Well, you sure know how to pan for gold," she said. "You must be very smart."

Sam blushed. "Oh, you don't have to be real smart to pan."

"How do you do it?" Phil blurted out. Angelica glared at him. But Sam didn't seem to mind.

"Well, you just shovel some dirt and gravel into your pan, like this." Grunting, Sam poked his shovel into the stony ground next to the river, stomped on it a few times, and finally dug out a little dirt, which he poured into his black metal pan.

"Next you add some water." He bent down to the river's edge and carefully scooped some water into the round pan.

"Like when we make mud pies!" said Lil.

"Then you swirl the water around," Sam continued, "and let a little bit slosh out over the edge. Gold is heavier than other rocks, so it stays at the bottom. Everything else gets washed out."

Holding the pan with both hands, Sam moved it around in a circle, slowly spilling the water out until there was none left. Then he peered at the bottom of the pan.

"How much gold is there?" asked Angelica.

"I want to see the gold!" said Lil, crowding next to Sam.

"There's none . . . again." Sam sighed. "I guess this isn't a very good spot. You're welcome to it, if you like." Sam picked up his shovel and walked away.

35

"Let's try it!" said Tommy, grabbing a pan out of Dil's stroller.

"Mine!" yelled Dil.

"I'm just going to use it for a minute, Dil," said Tommy. "Here's your rattle."

"Rad-o! Rad-o!" said Dil, delighted.

Tommy looked down to see if any ground looked like it had gold in it. It all looked the same—brown and rocky. He found a spot where no one else had dug, and scraped some dirt into the pan.

The others filled their pans, sand buckets, and sippy cups with dirt and rocks. Even Spike started to dig.

Tommy dipped his pan into the river. "Brrrr!" he said.

"This water's freezing!" said Susie.

Tommy tried to swirl the water around in the pan the way Sam had, but most of it spilled on him. He got more water and tried again. When he was done tipping the water out of the pan, there was a pebble sitting at the bottom.

"Is this gold?" asked Tommy, holding up the pebble.

Angelica squinted at it. "Nope. That's just a dumb old rock." None of the others had had any luck, either.

"Hmph," said Tommy, "panning for gold is hard."

"You oughta get yourself a cradle!" said a nearby prospector, whose name was Lotta.

"Yeah, a nap would be nice," said Phil, yawning.

"Not a sleeping cradle," Lotta said, "a *gold-washing* cradle, like this one." She pointed to a wooden box on rockers.

Lotta showed them how to put sand and gravel in the cradle, pour in water, and then rock the cradle back and forth until the heavy gold bits made their way down to a screen.

"With the cradle," she said, "you can search a lot faster than you can with a pan."

"Have you found any gold?" asked Susie.

"I surely have," Lotta said proudly. She opened a small pouch. They crowded around to look, and all they saw were a few tiny flakes of gold. They were not much bigger than grains of rice.

"That's it?" exclaimed Angelica.

"So you didn't find any big pieces of gold?" asked Tommy.

"Not around here," answered Lotta. "For that, you'd have to find the mother lode!"

Tommy nodded. "Up in the mountains, right?"

"That's what they say."

"Which way to the mountains?" asked Angelica eagerly.

Lotta pointed. "That way, up the river and past the town."

"What town?" asked Chuckie.

"It's so new, it doesn't have a name yet. But some people call it Bad Luck."

Bad Luck wasn't much of a town. Most people there lived in tents, and it had just one muddy street with a few stores along it. Headed for the mother lode in the mountains, Tommy and his fellow adventurers passed through, looking at the buildings.

One of the wooden buildings had a sign

with a picture of a bathtub on it. They saw a man inside paying with a pinch of gold dust. He stepped outside and slicked his wet hair back, looking clean as a whistle.

"'Scuse me," said Tommy, "can you tell me which way to the mountains, please?"

The clean man pointed down the street.

"Thanks," said Tommy. "Um, did you just buy a bathtub?"

He laughed. "No, I just bought a bath!"

Lil said, "You pay to take a bath?"

"Yep. And this place has the only tub in town," said the man. "'Course, round here most folks take a bath about once a week."

"This is a great place!" said Phil.

"They oughta call it Good Luck," said Lil.

As they walked along the street, they saw a place to get a haircut, a place to eat, and a place to buy digging tools. Then, near the end of the street, they heard music.

"Sounds like a band is playing," said Susie.

Tommy pointed at the last building in Bad Luck. "I think it's coming from over there."

Once they'd walked a little farther, they could

see through the front doors. Inside, lots of people were stomping their feet, listening to the musicians play, and watching girls dance in long, colorful dresses. The dancers were up on . . .

"A stage!" yelled Angelica, thrilled.

"Uh-huh," said Tommy. "And the guy said the mountains were this way . . ."

But Angelica didn't hear a word. She had already run inside and jumped up onto the stage.

CHAPTER 5

The dancers were surprised to see Angelica onstage with them. "What do you think you're doing?" one of them hissed at her.

"The Macaroona!" said Angelica. "Try to keep up."

Angelica elbowed her way to the center of the stage. She didn't dance like the other dancers, but she did dance in time with the music (mostly), crossing her arms in front of her, sticking them straight out, and then waving them over her head.

The audience just stared. Angelica was different from any dancer they'd seen before. Tommy, Chuckie, Susie, Phil, Lil, Dil, and even Spike ran into the room, but they all stayed at the back, watching.

"What is she doing?" Chuckie asked.

"Well, it's sort of like the Macarena," Susie said, "only different." She watched Angelica for a minute. "Real different."

The music changed. Hey, Angelica thought, I know this song.

Angelica danced over to one of the other dancers. "Psst," she whispered, "where's the microphone?"

"The what?" asked the dancer.

"Oh, never mind," said Angelica. "I'll just have to do without it."

She stepped up to the front of the stage, took a deep breath, and started to sing loudly:

"Oh, my starling
Oh, my starling
Oh, my staaaaaaaarling turpentine!
You're a frosted swan forever.
Won't you be my valentine?"

The dancers were horrified by Angelica's singing, but they kept dancing, hoping the audience would ignore her. But the audience's attention was on Angelica. They stared at her, wondering what her song meant. The musicians also started playing louder, trying to drown her out, but she simply sang even louder.

"In a cabinet, in a cannon
I was waaaaaaaiting for a sign,
Till a whiner in a diner
Fed cigars to Frankenstein!"

The dancers tried to push Angelica off the stage, but she dodged them and kept on singing. Spike started to howl.

"Oh, that snarling
Oh, that snarling
Oh, that snaaaaaaaarling dog of mine!
He should never, never ever
Try to bite a porcupine!"

Finally the musicians gave up trying to drown out Angelica and stopped playing. She took several bows and blew kisses to the audience.

"Thank you! Thank you!" Angelica called out, even though there was almost no applause.

After a few more bows, Angelica hopped off

the stage and ran over to Tommy and his friends. "So," she said, breathing hard, "what did you think?"

"Well," said Tommy, "um . . . Spike liked it!"

"Angelica, I don't think you're s'posed to sing in someone else's show," said Chuckie, worried.

"Why not?" demanded Angelica.

"They might get mad," Chuckie said.

"So what?" asked Angelica. "What are they gonna do, throw me in jail?"

Just then someone clamped his hand down on Angelica's shoulder. She gasped and stopped moving. Then, slowly turning around, she saw a big man wearing a shiny badge in front of her.

"Excuse me, miss—" he began to say.

Angelica's eyes grew wide. "Are—are you the sheriff?" she stammered.

"That's me," he said.

Suddenly Angelica cried out, "I didn't want to sing! They made me do it!" She pointed to the others. "It's not my fault! I want my lawyer! Oh, please don't put me in jail!"

"Who said anything about jail?" asked the sheriff. "I just wanted to tell you that there's a prospector on the other side of the room who wants to talk to you. See?"

The sheriff pointed. Across the room a man with a beard was waving. When he saw Angelica looking, he beckoned her over to his table.

"Oh." Angelica smiled. "Thanks, Mr. Sheriff!"

"Don't mention it," said the sheriff. He walked away.

Angelica turned to the others. "Wait here. I'm gonna go talk to this guy."

"But, Angelica," Susie said, "you don't even know who he is. We'll come with you."

"I may not know ezzackly who he is," Angelica said, "but I know ezzackly what he wants. He wants to make me a star!"

"Angelica, we're coming with you!" said Tommy.

"All right, all right," said Angelica impatiently. "Let's just go before he changes his mind!"

They all crossed the room together, squeezing between the crowded tables. Some of the customers glared at Angelica, still mad at her for the way she'd sung "Clementine."

But when Angelica reached the prospector's table, he smiled, and there were tears in his eyes. "Sit down, sit down," he said. "What's your name?"

"Angelica." She sat down, and the others stood around her.

"Angelica," he repeated. "Like an angel. A singing angel with golden hair."

"Thanks, mister."

"You can call me Orion. May I tell you something?

"Sure, Orion."

"When I first heard you sing, I thought to myself, 'Boy, this girl sure doesn't know the words to that song.'"

Angelica frowned. That wasn't what she wanted to hear from Orion.

He continued, "But when you got to the part about the snarling dog"—he paused a minute to swallow the lump in his throat—"and how that dog should never have bitten that porcupine, well I just . . ."

46

He turned aside a moment and sniffed. "Back east I used to have a dog like that, until he met up with a porcupine when we were out huntin' in the woods. Thinkin' about him again made me happy and sad all at the same time. And it helped me make up my mind. I'm giving up prospectin' in Californy and going back to Pennsylvania."

Orion took out a ragged handkerchief and blew his nose. Tommy and his friends just looked at each other. This guy had actually liked Angelica's weird song!

"Anyway," Orion said, taking a deep breath, "your song touched my heart, and I wanted to thank you."

"So you're not going to make me a star?" snapped Angelica.

Orion looked surprised. "Uh, no. How in tarnation would I do that?"

"Lotsa ways. Get me my own music place where everybody could come hear me sing, my own TV show. Put me in the movies."

"Movies?" Orion asked, frowning. "What's that?"

"Oh, forget it!" Angelica stood up.

"Now hold on," said Orion. "Don't run off just yet. You gave me the gift of your song—the first gift anyone's given me in a long time—and I would like to give you something in return."

"Well, it better be something good," Angelica said.

Orion thought a moment, then smiled. "Eureka! I've got it. Come with me." He started to leave the music hall. When he realized Angelica wasn't following him, he turned around. "Come on! Your friends, too."

"Should we go with him?" asked Lil.

"I might as well get something out of this," said Angelica, following Orion. The others looked at each other, then hurried to catch up.

As they left, a boy with his hat pulled low over his eyes got up and followed them.

They went outside, walked around the building, and climbed a small hill where several tents were pitched. Orion strode quickly to the farthest tent. "Just a minute," he said before ducking inside.

The walls of the tent glowed as Orion lit a

kerosene lamp. Then he stuck his head back out and invited them in. They all crowded into the canvas tent.

"Welcome to my humble home," he said. "Well, it's not my real home. That's in Pennsylvania, and I can't wait to get back there."

"Where is Pencil-vain-ya?" asked Tommy.

"It's a long way from here," said Orion, "a beautiful state, with hills and trees and—"

"Yeah, yeah, yeah," interrupted Angelica, "let's get to the presents."

Orion took his beat-up hat off, fumbled around the inner band, and fished out a key. Then he got down on his knees, reached under his cot, and pulled out a small box with a lock.

Angelica's eyes widened. "Golden treasure!" she whispered excitedly.

"Not exactly," said Orion, unlocking the box. He opened it, and they all leaned forward to see what was inside. The box was full of well-worn papers. It looked like they'd been folded and unfolded many, many times.

"There's nothing in here but papers!" said Angelica.

"What are those papers, Orion?" asked Susie. "Your homework?"

"These papers are a kind of treasure to me," he answered. "They're my letters from home."

"That's what you're giving me?" said Angelica, miffed. "A bunch of old letters?"

"Oh, no," said Orion. "I could never give these away. I have something else for you."

He took out a pocketknife, opened it, and pried the bottom off the wooden box. They all leaned forward again to see what was under the false bottom.

"Another paper?" said Angelica.

"Not just any paper," Orion said, "This is a map—well, half a map, anyway."

Suddenly Tommy thought he heard something rustle outside the tent. He listened again, but didn't hear anything.

"A map?" Angelica asked. "What kind of map?"

"A treasure map?" asked Phil eagerly.

"Exactly," said Orion. "It's half a map to the mother lode. I won it in a game. Unfortunately, I never found the other half of the map. I never found gold anywhere, either, so I'm going home. Here, you can have this map." He handed it to Angelica.

"Thanks, I guess," she said, disappointed.

"Yeah, thanks, Orion!" said Tommy.

"You're welcome," said Orion, smiling, "and I hope you have better luck than I've had."

"This is great!" said Tommy as they walked out of Orion's tent. "We can get lotsa gold to get lotsa Reptar Bars! We gots a map to the mother lode!"

"How do we read it, Tommy?" asked Chuckie.

"We just follow the line," said Tommy. "It's easy to read a map."

"Half a map," said Angelica, holding up the torn piece of paper.

"Alls we gotta do is find the other half," said Tommy.

"How are we s'posed to do that?" asked Lil.

"Well . . ." said Tommy, thinking.

But before he could say anything, someone sneaked up behind them and snatched the paper out of Angelica's hand!

"Hey!" yelled Angelica. "Give that back!"

They whirled around and saw a boy running away. His hat was pulled down low, and he had a handkerchief over his nose and mouth. With one hand holding the paper and the other holding on to his hat, he raced through the tents, back toward the town's only street.

"C'mon!" said Tommy, chasing after the thief.

"But it's dark!" Chuckie yelled after the others. "We might trip!" They all kept running, so Chuckie sighed and ran after them.

CHAPTER 6

With twice as many legs, Spike was the fastest runner. Tommy and his fellow shorty-niners didn't catch up with the bandit, but they could hear Spike barking far ahead of them. When they finally caught up with Spike, he was scratching at the back door of the store that sold digging tools.

"The robber must be in there!" said Susie. They tried to open the door, but it was locked.

"Let's see if there's another door," said Tommy, leading them to the front. The front door was locked, too, but they could see a light on inside through the window, so they knocked. There was no answer, so they knocked again. Still no answer. Angelica started banging on the door. Eventually they heard footsteps. A girl with dark brown hair opened the door just wide enough to stick her head out. "We're closed," she said, sounding annoyed.

"Let us in!" said Angelica. "There's a thief in there!"

"What?" asked the girl.

Talking fast, Tommy tried to explain. "Somebody stole our piece of paper and we tried to catch him but he got away except my dog Spike chased him right to this place so he must be inside." He took a deep breath.

"I don't know what you're babbling about," said the girl, "but I told you. We're closed!" She started to close the door, but Spike managed to squeeze through, pushing past the girl. He ran into the store, barking.

"Hey!" shouted the girl, chasing after Spike. "Dogs aren't allowed in here!"

Tommy and the others ran into the store. It was full of shovels, pickaxes, pans, sacks, ropes, boots, hats—everything a prospector could need.

But Tommy didn't stop to look. He followed the sound of Spike's growls to the back of the store, where the girl was tugging on his collar, trying to pull him away from a small door.

"What's behind that door?" asked Tommy.

"Just a little pantry. He must smell food," answered the girl. Spike stayed put, sniffing and growling at the crack under the door. "Now get this mutt out of here!"

"I will," said Tommy, "if you'll please just open that door."

"Fine!" said the girl. Tommy held on to Spike's collar while the girl opened the door.

And there was the thief, hiding under a shelf!

CHAPTER 7

"Persifer?" said the girl, obviously surprised.

"I was just, um, getting a little snack," said the boy in the pantry.

"You know him?" asked Susie.

"Of course I know him," answered the girl. "He's my brother."

"Give us back our map!" Angelica demanded.

"Map?" said the girl. "What map?"

"The map he stole!"

"I don't know what they're talking about, Penelope," said the boy. "I didn't steal anything." He held out his hands for everyone to see. They were empty.

"I'm going to look!" declared Angelica, pulling the boy out of the pantry. She stepped inside and started hunting for the map.

Penelope said, "If you break anything in there, you'll have to pay for it!" Her brother, Persifer, looked nervous.

"I found it!" shouted Angelica, as she tugged the half-map out from under a wooden crate. Angelica waved the map triumphantly over her head. "See?" she said to Penelope, "I told you he stole it!"

Penelope stared at the paper Angelica was holding. "Wait a minute," she said, "that's mine!"

"No, it isn't," said Susie, "it's ours!"

"That's right!" added Tommy. "Orion gave it to us!"

"To me," Angelica corrected.

"I'll prove to you it's mine." Penelope ran into another room, and came back with a torn piece of paper. When she held it up to the half-map, the jagged edges of the two pieces of paper matched perfectly!

"It's the other half of my map!" cried Angelica.

"No," said Penelope, "the paper you're holding is the other half of my map." She turned to her brother. "Persifer, where did you get it?"

"I told you," said Angelica, "he stole it from me."

Penelope folded her arms and glared at her brother. "Persifer?"

Persifer looked at the angry faces around him. "All right, all right. I'll tell you what happened."

"Good," said Penelope. "Tell the truth."

"Remember when you tore the map in two and gave me half, saying that'd be safer than leaving the whole map in one place?"

"Of course."

"Well, I lost my half in a game."

Penelope looked mad. "Who did you lose it to?"

"A prospector," said Persifer.

"That was Orion," said Tommy.

Persifer nodded. "I watched him for a long time, trying to get the map back, but there was never a chance, until he gave it to you." He looked at Angelica. "Then I took it, so I could give it back to my sister."

"But if the map is yours," Susie asked Penelope, "where did you get it from in the first place?"

"A girl from one of the local tribes—the Miwok—traded it for some cloth. She'd found

58

the map, but her family needed cloth more than they needed gold."

"She probably didn't want any Reptar Bars," Chuckie whispered to Tommy.

"How did you know the map was real, and not just a fake?" asked Angelica.

"I know that girl would not lie," Penelope said. "If she said that the map leads to the mother lode, then it must be so."

Phil scratched his head. "If you had a map to the mother lode, why didn't you go get the gold?"

"We tried," said Penelope, sighing.

"It's not easy," added Persifer, "especially for just two people. Once we got up in the mountains, it started snowing really hard, and we lost the trail."

"We thought about trying to go on, but then I saw big tracks in the snow. Grizzly tracks," said Penelope.

"Drizzly tracks?" wondered Phil.

"I think they gots something to do with rain," said Lil.

"Not drizzly, *grizzly*," said Persifer, "as in

grizzly bear, the biggest, meanest bear there is."

"Then that was smart," said Chuckie.

"What was?" asked Penelope.

"Turning around and coming back," said Chuckie, shuddering at the thought of a big, mean bear.

Angelica was getting impatient. She had her half of the map back, so she was ready to leave. "Well, it's been nice talking to you. See you later!" She turned to go.

"Wait!" called Penelope. "You've still got half of the map."

"That's right," Angelica said, "because I sang a beautiful song, and Orion liked it and he gave me a present. Bye."

"But half a map's no good." Penelope ran to the front door and blocked the way.

"Cynthia and I will figure it out somehow," said Angelica. "Now get out of our way."

Penelope stood there, thinking. "Look," she said, "half a map is worthless. But with a whole map, we could all go together, and there'd be plenty of gold for everyone. . . ."

"I don't know," said Angelica, hesitating. "I

need, I mean *we* need a lot of gold."

"Just enough to buy some Reptar Bars, Angelica," said Chuckie.

"Chuckie, be quiet!" Angelica snapped.

Penelope went on. "We could use equipment and food from our store . . ."

"Food sounds good," said Phil, whose tummy had been growling. "Got any Dummi Bears?"

Penelope looked at him. "No," she said, "we don't eat bears."

Phil was about to explain, but Penelope had turned away. "You could sleep on blankets here in the store tonight," she told everyone, "and we'll head for the mountains tomorrow."

Lil yawned. She was getting sleepy.

"Let's do it, Angelica!" said Tommy. "Let's stick the two pieces together and all go as one big group of shorty-niners!"

"Penelope's right," Susie said, "a whole map is way better than half a map."

Angelica sighed. She hated to agree with Susie, but what she said made sense. Without the other half of the map, they might never find any gold at all. "All right," she said, "but I'm still holding on to my half."

"Agreed," said Penelope. "We'll leave in the morning. And this time, we'll have the fire-haired boy with us." She looked at Chuckie.

Tommy was surprised. "You know that story too?"

Penelope smiled. "With your redheaded friend along, we're sure to find the mother lode."

The other babies all cheered, except for Chuckie. He was still thinking about grizzly bears.

CHAPTER 8

Chuckie was walking through the snow. Suddenly he tripped and fell. He stood up, brushed off the snow, and looked down. He was standing in a giant footprint!

I gots to get out of here, he thought. He started to climb out of the huge footprint. Then a shadow fell across the snow. *Roar!* Right behind Chuckie was the biggest bear he'd ever seen! Chuckie scrambled out of the footprint and started to run. Just as the bear was about to catch him, Reptar stomped into view!

"Yay!" Chuckie cheered. "Reptar will save me!"

With a mighty roar Reptar leaped at the gigantic bear. But the bear easily picked Reptar up, spun him around over his head, and tossed him off a cliff!

"Oh, no!" screamed Chuckie. "Reptaaaaar!"

Persifer shook Chuckie's shoulder. "Wake up! Wake up!" Chuckie sat up and rubbed his eyes. He was still in the store, and the sun was shining through the window. "You were yelling in your sleep," Persifer said. "I think you were having a nightmare about tar."

Penelope came into the room. "Get up, everyone! Breakfast is ready. I made flapjacks." She went back into the kitchen behind the store.

"Flapjacks?" said Tommy. "What are flapjacks?"

"I dunno," Lil said, stretching. "But they smell good."

Everybody got up and went into the kitchen, and Penelope handed them plates of food. "Oh, pancakes!" said Tommy.

After breakfast they got ready to go. Penelope packed lots of food, including flour, grease, sugar, dried apples, beef, potatoes, beans, bacon, salt pork, and pickles.

They filled a small wagon with the food, camping equipment, and tools to dig for gold. It reminded Tommy of the red wagon he had in his backyard, only bigger.

"Maybe your dog could pull the wagon," Persifer suggested.

"No, we've done that," Tommy said. "Spike

just goes where he wants to go. And when he runs, everything falls out."

"Spike needs a steering wheel," said Susie.

"And brakes," added Angelica.

When everything was ready, Penelope hung a CLOSED sign in the front window of the store and locked the door. Then she and Angelica held their two halves of the map together. "I remember the first part of the trip from the other time we tried it," Penelope said, "but we didn't get very far. Come on, we begin on this path."

They started walking. "Who made you the boss of everything?" Angelica muttered to herself, watching Penelope lead the way.

Soon the path started to wind up into the mountains. The pine trees smelled nice, and the little waterfalls were pretty, but it wasn't easy pulling the wagon and pushing Dil in his stroller. "I told you we should've left him behind," Angelica complained.

"But, Angelica," Tommy said, "if Dil hadn't come along, who would've tricked that rattle-snake?"

"Your baby brother did that?" Persifer asked, astonished.

"Yup," said Tommy proudly.

"Here," said Persifer, "let me push him."

"Up, up, up, up, up," said Dil.

They couldn't go very fast. Sometimes they had to cross over streams, and in some places trees had fallen across the path.

Suddenly Chuckie yelled, "Augghh! A bug flew right in my face!"

"Boy," said Phil, "he gets all the luck."

"That's 'cause he's got the hairs like fire," said Lil knowingly.

Chuckie wiped his glasses, and they kept on hiking.

"We'll follow this trail until we come to Antelope Rock," said Penelope, looking at her half of the map.

"Cantaloupe Rock?" said Lil. "Mmm."

Persifer shook his head. "Not Cantaloupe Rock, *Antelope* Rock. The rock looks a little like an antelope."

"Is that it?" asked Susie, pointing ahead. There was a big rock by the trail that looked like a deer, with two jagged parts like antlers.

"That's it!" said Penelope. "This is where we leave the trail, and the going gets a little rough."

"You mean it's been easy so far?" muttered Angelica.

Later in the afternoon, it started to get cool and the shorty-niners were beginning to shiver.

"Brrrr!" said Chuckie.

"It is a little bit chilly," admitted Susie.

They had pulled the wagon and the stroller over some big rocks, when Lil spotted something on the ground. "Hey, look," she said, "a doggie pawprint!"

Spike sniffed the pawprint, and then stepped in it. His pawprint was a lot smaller than the one on the ground!

"Must have been an awfully big dog," said Phil.

Persifer knelt down by the print. "A dog didn't make this."

"Shh!" said Penelope to her brother. "You'll only scare them."

"Why should we be scared of a hole in the dirt?" asked Tommy. He put his hand in the pawprint and patted the ground.

"She means we'll be scared of what made that footprint," said Angelica.

"Why?" asked Phil. "Did a ghost make it?"

"Or a monster?" added Lil.

"Or the G-Gold M-M-Man?" asked Chuckie.

"Don't be ridiculous!" said Penelope. "Ghosts don't leave footprints, there aren't any monsters up here, and I've never heard of such a thing as the Gold Man!"

"Then what made the footprint, Penelope?" asked Tommy. "You can tell us. We won't be scared."

Penelope hesitated, then sighed. "This is the footprint of a grizzly bear."

"Grizzly bear?" yelled Chuckie. "Auuugggh!"

"Don't worry," said Persifer, "if a grizzly bear comes around, we'll give him our bacon."

"What'll that do?" asked Chuckie.

"Make him even hungrier," said Angelica. "It's called an app-uh-teaser."

"Come on, let's move on," Penelope said.

They followed her up the mountain.

Well, thought Chuckie as he looked back at the footprint, at least it's not as big as the one in my dream.

CHAPTER 9

As the afternoon wore on, everyone started to get a little cranky. Angelica said they were going too slow. Lil said they were going too fast. Phil said he was hungry.

"I've got an idea," said Penelope, handing Phil part of a dried apple, "let's sing a song while we walk. That'll make the hike go faster."

"Good idea, Penelope," said Tommy.

"You start us off, Persifer," Penelope told her brother.

"All right." Persifer thought a minute, and then sang:

> "Oh, I'm standin' in the river
> And the water sure is cold,
> But I'll stand all day and freeze all night
> To get a lump of gold.
>
> "California,
> Yes, that's the land for me.

70

I am bound for California
With a washbowl on my knee."

"Hey, I know that song!" said Lil as she stepped over a fallen branch. "But it was about someone with a banjo on his knee."

"I've got a boo-boo on my knee," said Phil proudly.

"Out here the prospectors sing it all the time," said Persifer, "and the words are always about hunting for gold."

"Let me try!" said Lil. "Um . . ."

"When you pan for gold you get to watch
The water splash and squirt.
But I'd rather dig for gold because
I get to play in dirt."

Then they all sang:

California,
Yes, that's the land for me.
I am bound for California
With a washbowl on my knee."

"My turn!" said Angelica.

71

"If you see a pile of shinin' gold,
You might say "ooh" and "aah."
But there's somethin' much more beautiful—
Her name's Angelica."

Then everyone sang again:

"California,
Yes, that's the land for me.
I am bound for California
With a washbowl on my knee."

"Hey, this is fun!" said Chuckie. "I'll try one!" But just as he was about to sing, Spike started howling.

"It's Chuckie's turn, Spike!" said Susie.

But Spike kept howling. And barking. And growling. Tommy tried to calm him down, but Spike kept on making about as much noise as one dog could.

"What's the matter, Spike?" asked Tommy.

"Maybe your dog doesn't like music," said Persifer.

"No . . ." said Tommy.

"Maybe he saw a squirrel," Phil suggested.

72

"No . . ."

Staring at a thick clump of trees just ahead, Spike kept on growling, barking, and howling.

Chuckie said, "Maybe Spike smells something in those . . . AUUUUUGGGGH!"

Turning to see what Chuckie was looking at, their mouths fell open—it was a grizzly bear!

CHAPTER 10

The huge bear stood up on its hind legs and sniffed the air. Everyone started to run, but Penelope cried out, "Don't run! He'll just chase us! Quick, climb a tree! I'll take Dil!"

The grizzly dropped down onto all four feet and came toward them. He wasn't growling; he just seemed curious, sniffing the air.

"What about Spike?" asked Tommy.

"I'll carry him," said Persifer. "Just climb!"

Luckily, there were lots of pine trees with low branches they could reach. They scrambled up into the trees as the bear followed them. With Spike in one arm, Persifer just barely managed to swing into a tree before the grizzly reached them. Spike kept barking and growling.

When the bear stood up, it could reach pretty far up the tree trunks, so they climbed higher. Chuckie felt dizzy. "Do grizzly bears climb trees?" he asked, his voice shaking.

"They don't much like to, from what I've heard," said Persifer, struggling to hold on to a squirming Spike, "and they're probably too heavy for these branches."

"I hope *we're* not too heavy," Susie said.

"Get out of here, you stupid ugly bear!" Angelica shouted.

But the bear didn't leave. First it went from tree to tree, reaching as high as it could and sniffing.

Next it looked in Dil's stroller.

"Mine!" yelled Dil.

Spike growled at the bear.

"Maybe we can scare away the bear with these pine cream cones," said Tommy. He broke one off and threw it at the bear. It hit the bear's furry back and bounced off. The bear didn't even notice. Then it started sniffing around the wagon with the food.

"Maybe if he eats all our food, he'll be too full to eat us," said Phil hopefully.

"Like when we eat so many worms, and we don't want s'getti," said Lil.

"Didn't you two hear what I said before

about an app-uh-teaser?" asked Angelica.

Spike was still growling at the bear. Suddenly Spike kicked and squirmed so hard that Persifer almost fell out of the tree!

Slipping, Persifer grabbed for a branch, but as he caught it, he dropped Spike!

Snarling and showing his teeth, Spike fell to the ground and scrambled onto his feet. The bear, who had just pulled a slab of bacon out of the wagon, dropped it and turned toward Spike. Spike barked at him. Everyone held their breath. The grizzly bear lifted a giant paw to strike at the dog.

"Be careful, Spike!" Tommy cried.

Spike looked up at Tommy and then pulled back, running into the woods. The dog knew that he had to get the bear away from Tommy and his friends. The grizzly followed Spike through the trees until neither of them could be seen. A minute passed, and then they couldn't even be heard. The woods were silent.

"Spike!" Tommy called. "Spike, come back!"

"But don't bring the bear with you!" called Angelica.

"Hurry," said Persifer, starting to climb down, "let's get out of here before the grizzly comes back." Then he turned to Tommy and said, "Your dog is very brave. He ran away so the bear wouldn't hurt us."

Tommy nodded.

Penelope started to climb down too. "According to the map, there's an old cabin not too far from here. We can spend the night there."

"But what about Spike?" asked Tommy. "We have to wait for him to come back!"

"I'm not waiting here for a bear to come back and eat me 'cause of some smelly old dog," said Angelica.

"He's not smelly!" said Tommy. "And he's not old! He's my dog!"

"The cabin's in the direction Spike ran. We can follow him and head for the cabin at the same time."

"Don't worry, Tommy," said Lil, "we'll find Spike!"

"Yeah!" said Phil. "We've followed him around the yard lots of times."

"And if we don't find him," Susie added,

"he'll find us. Remember the time Spike ran away for a long time, but then he came home?"

"Yeah . . ." said Tommy, "but he knows where our house is. How's he s'posed to know where we are up here?"

"Dogs' noses are lots better than ours," Susie said. "He'll smell us. And our food."

"And so will the bear," Angelica muttered.

Everyone climbed down from the trees, gathered up the wagon and the stroller, and hurried toward the cabin. Along the way, they kept an eye out for Spike, but they didn't see him.

They reached the old cabin just before dark. It was made out of tree trunks that still had the bark on, and the floor was bare dirt.

"This is the dirtiest place I've ever seen!" exclaimed Angelica.

"Yeah, isn't it great?" said Phil.

They ate some food, but Tommy wasn't hungry. He couldn't stop thinking about Spike. He wondered where his dog was, if the bear was still chasing him, and if Spike was getting hungry.

Suddenly a drop of water fell on Tommy's head—*plop!*

"Hey," said Tommy, "who dripped water on my head?"

"Why would we do that?" answered Chuckie. Just then a big drop fell on Chuckie's head. "Hey! That's wet!"

Angelica laughed at Chuckie. "Yeah, Chuckie, drops of water usually are wet." She laughed again, until three drops fell on her head—*plink, plonk, ploonk!*

"Where's all this water coming from?" yelled Angelica. She looked up and saw lots of drips about to fall from the ceiling.

"It's raining inside the house!" Lil cried.

"No," said Susie, looking out the small window, "it's raining outside. And the roof leaks."

She was right. The roof was very leaky, and now the rain was pouring down hard.

Everyone tried to find a spot in the little cabin that wasn't wet, but water had leaked through the roof almost everywhere. They ended up huddled together in one corner.

"Lil!" said Angelica, "get your foot out of my face!"

"Your elbow is poking me!" said Lil.

"Phil," Susie said, "stop digging; it's time to sleep!"

"But you can dig for worms without even going outside!" said Phil.

There was barely room for anyone to turn around without getting wet, but at least sleeping close together helped keep them warm. As the night went on, the temperature dropped quickly.

Tommy lay awake for a long time, wondering where Spike was spending such a wet and cold night.

CHAPTER 11

When they woke up, it still felt cold, but the sun was shining through the window.

"Hey, it's not raining anymore!" said Susie.

"That's good," said Penelope. "It wouldn't be much fun hiking in the rain."

Angelica got up, stretched, and walked over to the little window. She peered out and was surprised at what she saw. "Look, you guys!" she shouted. Angelica ran to open the door.

"Wow!" Phil exclaimed.

"Snow!" said Tommy.

Outside, everything was white. During the night, the rain had turned to snow!

"Up here it can snow anytime," explained Penelope. "I hope it's not too deep."

It wasn't. When they went outside, the snow didn't even come up to the tops of their shoes, except where the wind had blown it into drifts.

Tommy cupped his hands to his mouth and called, "Spike!" His voice echoed down the mountain, but no barks came bouncing back.

"Are these Spike's feetprints?" asked Phil. Tommy ran over to where Phil was looking at the snow-covered ground.

"No," said Tommy, disappointed. "They're too big to be Spike's."

"Are they more grizzly bear tracks?" asked Chuckie, scared.

Persifer knelt down to look at the prints more closely. "No," he said, "these aren't grizzly tracks."

"Whew," said Chuckie, relieved.

"They're *mountain lion* tracks," said Persifer.

"LION?" yelled Chuckie. "AUUGGHHH!"

"Let's get out of here," said Penelope.

Chuckie ran back into the cabin, and the others followed. They quickly put on their warmest clothes, packed up, and headed out.

Chuckie was the last one to peek out the door of the cabin. "Do you see the lion any-where?"

"No, Chuckie," said Tommy, "and I still don't see Spike."

"Don't worry, Tommy," Chuckie assured him, "I know Spike's gonna come back."

"Angelica," said Penelope, "let's put the maps together."

"I'm getting pretty tired of you bossing me around all the time," said Angelica. "Maybe I don't feel like putting the maps together."

"Then tell me, Miss Angelica," said Penelope, getting angry, "what do you feel like doing?"

Angelica stood there, thinking.

"We could build a snowman," suggested Lil helpfully.

"Lil," said Susie, "this is no time to build a snowman."

"Okay . . ." said Lil, "let's build a snow lady."

"C'mon, Angelica," said Susie, "let's get outta here before the mountain lion comes back!"

"Well," Angelica said to Penelope, "this time instead of me holding my half of the map up to your half . . ."

"Yes?" asked Penelope, waiting.

"You hold your half of the map up to my half!"

"What's the difference?" whispered Phil to Lil. Lil shrugged.

"Fine!" said Penelope. Angelica's stubbornness was annoying, but they really needed to get going, and without both halves of the map, she didn't know which way they should go. Penelope held her half of the map up to Angelica's.

"Where are we now?" asked Angelica.

"Right outside the cabin," said Tommy.

"I mean, where are we on the map?"

Penelope pointed to the wrinkled paper. "Here's the cabin . . . so we want to go that way." She pointed toward a big pile of rocks.

"Oh, boy," said Lil unenthusiastically, "more rocks to climb."

As the sun rose higher in the sky, and it got warmer, the snow began to melt. The wet ground was slippery, and Chuckie fell more than once. He wasn't always watching where he was going, because he was keeping an eye out for bears and lions.

Later that day Chuckie noticed that Tommy was trailing behind. He waited for Tommy to catch up. "Hey, Tommy, whatcha lookin' out for? A mountain lion?"

"Nope."

"A grizzly bear?"

"Nope."

"A rattlesnake?"

"Nope."

"Then what, Tommy?"

"A dog," said Tommy sadly.

"Uh-oh," said Penelope, stopping. They had come to the edge of a mountain stream. With all the melting snow, it was full of cold water that was moving quite fast.

"Can we go around it?" asked Susie.

"I don't think so," said Penelope. For as far as they could see in both directions, the stream stretched on and on. It was too wide to jump across and it looked too deep to walk across.

"Did we bring a boat?" asked Phil.

"Sure, Phil," said Angelica sarcastically, "I've

got one in my pocket."

"Great!" said Phil. "I wanna ride in front!"

"She's just teasing, Phil," explained Susie. "We don't have a boat."

"Oh," said Phil, disappointed.

The water churned and splashed as they looked for stepping-stones, but there weren't any.

"We could make a boat," said Persifer.

"How?" asked Susie.

"Well," he answered, "there's lots of big logs on the ground. Maybe we could use them."

Tommy cheered up a little. "Great idea, Persifer!"

"I brought rope," added Persifer. "We could tie two logs together and make a raft."

"Yeah," said Susie, "let's do it!"

Close to the creek, they found two logs big enough for all of them. Grunting and groaning, everyone pushed and pushed, rolling the two logs next to each other. Then Persifer lashed the logs together with his rope. "There," he said. "It's not a real boat, but it should be good enough to get us across."

Straining again, they shoved the raft into

the water, leaving one end on the bank of the stream, and holding on tight so the current wouldn't pull it away. Carefully they scooted onto the logs. Persifer got on last. He and Penelope held big sticks to push and steer with. "Here we go!" he cried, pushing them out into the water.

The rapidly flowing stream took the raft right away, and started to sweep it down the mountain. But Persifer and Penelope pushed hard with their sticks, and everyone else paddled with their hands, aiming for the other side of the stream.

"Wheeeee!" cried Phil and Lil.

"YAAAAAAAAH!" screamed Chuckie.

They had almost reached the other side when the raft hit a big rock that was just under the surface of the water! *Crash!* The raft swung around, and the ropes came loose. The two logs quickly came apart!

"HELP!" yelled Chuckie.

Now both logs were floating down the swollen stream. Pushing against the bottom of the stream with their sticks, Penelope and

Persifer got their log over to the other side. Dripping wet, the brother and sister crawled onto the bank, followed by Angelica, Phil, and Lil. Some of their food had fallen in the water, but they still had the wagon.

Panting, Persifer asked, "Did the others reach the bank yet?"

Shading his eyes with his hand, Phil looked down the stream. "Uh-uh."

Far downstream, Phil could see Tommy, Chuckie, Susie, and Dil still holding on tightly to the other log. Suddenly they went around a bend—and disappeared!

CHAPTER 12

"We're doooooomed!" yelled Chuckie over the roar of the water.

"Hold on!" Tommy yelled back. With one hand he was clutching a knob on the log, and with the other he was holding on to Dil's stroller. The wheels were jammed into the log.

Susie was holding on to Dil too. She was also kicking her feet in the water, trying to steer the log over to the bank. Dil was laughing and clapping his hands.

"I'm scared!" cried Chuckie.

"Don't be scared, Chuckie," Susie told him. "Pretend you're on a ride at the water park!"

"That's scary too!" Chuckie wailed.

"Look!" said Tommy, glancing down the stream. They were headed for a big rock!

"Uh-oh," said Susie.

The front end of the log bumped into the rock—hard, but not hard enough to bump them off the log. It got caught in a little notch in the rock, and the back end swung around.

"Whoa!" yelled Chuckie, holding on as tightly as he could. There were drips of water on his glasses, and his hair was soaked.

The back end of the log got caught on an even bigger rock. Now they were stuck between two rocks.

"Now what are we going to do?" Chuckie moaned. "We'll have to live on this log forever."

"No, we won't," Susie told him. "We can crawl onto that big rock."

"And then what?" asked Chuckie. "Live on a big rock forever?"

"We'll figure that out when we get there," Susie said. "Come on!"

Moving slowly and carefully, they crawled onto the boulder. Susie pushed Dil's stroller in front of her.

But Dil wasn't happy about getting off the log. He wanted to keep riding on the water. "No! No! No! No!" he yelled.

"Yes, Dil!" said Tommy. "We're getting on the rock." Just as Tommy crawled onto the rock, the water swept the log down the stream. It hit a boulder and broke in two!

"Boy," said Tommy, "that was close!"

"It's good we got off that log," Chuckie said, "but now we're stuck on this rock!"

Susie looked around. "Hey, this side of the rock is pretty close to the grass," she said, pointing.

Chuckie and Tommy saw that the bank of the stream was only about three feet away.

"I don't think I can jump that far," said Chuckie.

"Me either," said Tommy.

They stared at the water between the big rock and the bank. It looked deep, and it was moving very quickly.

"I've got an idea," said Susie. "Tommy, take Dil out of his stroller, please."

Tommy lifted Dil out. After a few tries Susie got the stroller to fold up. Then, holding the wheels, she dropped the stroller across the gap between the rock and the stream bank. The curved handles hooked over a tree root on the bank.

"Good idea, Susie! Dil's stroller is a little bridge!" Tommy said.

"I'll go first to test it out," Susie said. "If you put Dil on my back, will he hold on?"

"I think so," answered Tommy. "When my dad plays 'horsey' with him, he says Dil holds on so tight, he could ride a bunkin' bongo."

Tommy got Dil onto Susie's back. "Horsey, Dil, horsey!" Tommy said to his baby brother.

Dil giggled. "Ossy! Ossy!" he called out as he wrapped his arms around Susie's neck.

"Okay," said Susie, "here goes. Hold on to this end of the stroller."

Tommy and Chuckie held on. Susie carefully crawled across the stroller as Dil giggled.

"She made it!" said Tommy.

Susie put Dil down and held the other end of the stroller. "You're next, Chuckie," she said. "Then Tommy."

"Okay," said Chuckie, shaking a little.

"You can do it, Chuckie!" Susie called.

Chuckie got down on his hands and knees. He crawled to the edge of the big rock and looked down into the water. He shuddered.

"Don't look at the water, Chuckie," Susie called, "look at me." She smiled at him.

Chuckie felt a little better and took a deep breath. "All right," he said, "here I go." Slowly Chuckie crawled out onto the stroller and then, inch by inch, made his way across to the grass.

"Yay!" yelled Tommy. "Way to go, Chuckie!"

"I knew you could do it," said Susie.

"Good old grass," Chuckie said, lying on the ground, "I could kiss you." Just then a tiny lizard ran in front of his face. "Yaaah!" he yelled, jumping up.

"Okay, Tommy," shouted Susie over the roar of the water, "it's your turn!" She held one handle of the stroller, and Chuckie got down to hold the other. Dil waved to his big brother.

Tommy crawled out onto the stroller. When he was more than halfway across, the wheels behind him suddenly slipped into the water!

Tommy threw himself forward, and Susie let go of the stroller to catch his hands. Chuckie held on to the other handle, using all his might to keep the stroller from being swept down the stream.

Tommy's feet got soaked, but Susie pulled him onto the bank. Then they helped Chuckie pull the stroller up. They did it!

Dil clapped his hands and laughed. Susie lifted him into his stroller, and they were ready to go. But where?

"Maybe if we walk back up this side," Tommy said, "we'll find everybody."

"Yeah, and Spike will be there waiting for us," said Susie, trying to sound sure of what she was saying. Tommy's face brightened.

But they saw that this side of the stream was lined with thick bushes and piles of rocks.

"I don't think we can walk up this way," Chuckie said.

"Then we'll just have to go around," Tommy told him. "Come on!" Pushing Dil's stroller, he set off into the woods, followed by Susie and Chuckie.

CHAPTER 13

"Do you see 'em?" called Lil to her brother.

Phil was up on a rock, looking down the stream. "No," said Phil. "But I saw a lizard."

"Did you catch it?" asked Lil.

"Oh, come on," Angelica said impatiently. "Let's just go. We know which way they went."

"There's lots of bushes and rocks here," Phil said as he slid down from the boulder.

"We'll have to go away from the stream and then keep working our way back to it, checking to see if they've climbed out," said Penelope. "Angelica, do you still have your half of the map?"

Angelica held up a slightly damp piece of paper. "I've got mine. Have you got yours?"

"Right here," said Penelope, holding up her half. "Let's go."

She headed away from the stream, and Persifer started to follow, pulling the wagon.

The wagon was lighter now, as some things had fallen into the stream.

"Boy, Penelope sure is bossy," Angelica said to Lil. "I can't stand bossy people."

"Oh," said Lil, "I'm used to it."

They started to go, but something across the stream caught Phil's eye. "Hey," he said, "what's that?"

They all turned to look. Coming out of the trees on the other side of the creek was the biggest cat they'd ever seen!

Persifer whispered, "That's a mountain lion. Probably the one who made those tracks we saw."

The light brown mountain lion walked slowly to the edge of the stream and began to drink.

Penelope whispered, "Be very quiet. Don't let it know we're here."

The mountain lion kept on drinking. "It drinks just like my cat, Fluffy," Angelica whispered. She took a step to see better, and put her foot on a dry twig. *Snap!* The mountain lion stopped drinking and looked up. It seemed to be looking right at Angelica, Phil, Lil, Penelope, and Persifer.

"Do you think it heard that?" Angelica asked, still whispering.

"Yes," said Penelope.

"Do you think it sees us?"

"Yes."

"Do you think it can jump over the stream?"

"I . . . I'm not sure."

"Well," said Angelica, "I'm not sticking around to find out!" She turned and ran as fast as her legs could carry her. The twins ran after her.

Penelope and Persifer looked at each other. Penelope followed the twins. Persifer tossed some food onto the ground, hoping to slow down the mountain lion. Then he ran after Penelope, pulling the wagon behind him.

"Are we going the right way, Tommy?" asked Susie. It was confusing walking through the woods. They had to make up their own trails.

"I think so," answered Tommy.

"Which way is the river?" asked Chuckie.

"That way," said Tommy and Susie at the same time, pointing in different directions.

Chuckie looked at Tommy and Susie. "We're lost! Spike's lost! What are we gonna do?"

Tommy tried to be brave. "We're not lost, Chuckeroo!" he said. "We're just . . . um . . . a little mixed up."

They kept walking until they reached a mountain meadow—a place where there weren't so many trees, and the ground was covered with long grass instead of rocks.

"This is a nice place, isn't it?" said Susie. She headed farther into the meadow.

Following her, Chuckie looked around. "It's nice, I guess, but I still don't see the river."

"Ossy! Ossy!" said Dil.

"No, Dil, I am not going to carry you on my back," Susie said.

"Ossy! Ossy!" Dil pointed toward the far side of the meadow.

"Hey," cried Tommy, "Dil's right! There is a horse! And it's running over here!"

But it wasn't just one horse running toward them. It was a herd of wild horses galloping across the meadow—a stampede!

The mountain lion leaned back on its hind legs, then sprang forward, leaping across the stream. It sniffed the food Persifer had dropped, then trotted on, following the scent it had smelled back by the cabin.

Lil was running as fast as she could to catch up with Angelica. "I'm running . . . out of . . . bread again," she panted.

Phil was running alongside Penelope and Persifer. "Do you think that mountain lion is chasing us?" he asked.

Just then they heard a growl.

"I would say yes," Persifer said.

They ran faster, until all five of them were running side by side, with the wagon clattering along behind them.

As she ran, Angelica pulled Cynthia out of her backpack. "Sorry, Cynthia," she said, "but if the mountain lion tries to eat me, I'm gonna throw you at him."

"But Angelica," Lil said, shocked, "Cynthia is

your mostest bestest friend!"

"She is," Angelica answered, "and that's why she's going to fight the lion for me."

They kept running, but the mountain lion was quickly gaining on them. Suddenly the adventurers broke out of the trees into a meadow.

"Look!" shouted Persifer. "There are the others!"

Angelica, Persifer, Penelope, Phil, and Lil arrived at the meadow just as Tommy spotted the stampede of wild horses.

"Those horses are coming right at us!" Susie yelled. They were trying to decide which way to run, when Chuckie saw Angelica and the others in the meadow. He jumped up and down.

"They're here!" he yelled.

"Not yet, but they will be any second," Susie said, thinking that Chuckie was talking about the horses.

"No, not the horses! It's Phil and Lil! And Penelope and Persifer! And Angelica!"

The two groups of shorty-niners ran toward

each other. But the horses were still coming their way.

"A stampede!" cried Persifer.

Dust was flying under the horses' hooves. As they came closer, their galloping sounded like thunder.

"Horses!" shouted Angelica. "I love horses! But those are coming a little too fast."

"They're gonna run right over us!" yelled Lil.

Just as the horses were about to reach the shorty-niners, the mountain lion leaped into the meadow. When the horses saw it, they turned and headed away from the babies.

"Yay!" said Susie. "The horses are going away!"

"Yeah," said Angelica, "but the lion's still here!"

She was right. The mountain lion turned toward the babies. Chuckie closed his eyes, fearing the worst. Suddenly a shadow cut quickly across the clearing, then jumped in between the lion and the babies!

CHAPTER 14

"Spike!" everyone exclaimed. Tommy wanted to run up and hug his dog, but the mountain lion's growl kept him back. Spike took a step toward the lion.

"No, Spike!" yelled Tommy. He was excited to see his dog again, but worried that the mountain lion would hurt him. "Stay away from that kitty!"

Spike didn't run at the mountain lion, but stayed in between the big cat and the babies, barking and growling. His lips curled back, and he showed his sharpest teeth.

Then, just when it looked like the mountain lion was about to spring at Spike, something whizzed through the air and whacked the lion—right on the nose! It was Cynthia! The mountain lion looked stunned for a second, then ran away.

Everyone cheered. "Angelica," said Tommy,

"you threw Cynthia and helped save Spike!"

"That was a great throw!" cried Phil.

"Well, I am one of the world's bestest throwers," Angelica said, running over to find Cynthia.

"You threw your bestest friend to save Spike!" said Lil.

"He may be kind of a stinky dog, but he's all right sometimes," admitted Angelica. "Besides, Cynthia's tougher than any stupid mountain lion! Where are you, Cynthia?"

Angelica searched through the high grass and finally found Cynthia. "Good job, Cynthia," she whispered to the doll. As usual, Cynthia didn't say anything.

Tommy ran over to hug Spike. Everyone else came over to pet Spike, telling him what a good dog he was.

Tired from all the excitement, everyone sat at the edge of the meadow under a tall tree, eating and talking. Spike lay with his head in Tommy's lap. Tommy scratched his dog behind the ears. Penelope and Angelica studied the map to the mother lode. "I think I've figured out where we are on the map," Penelope said. "The mother lode isn't far."

"Good," said Lil, "'cause I'm tired."

"Just think of all the Reptar Bars we're gonna get with the gold, Lil," Phil said.

"Yeah," said Lil. "Five!"

"Millions!" cried Phil.

"Gajillions!" yelled Lil. And the twins fell back, laughing.

They were walking through a narrow, rocky canyon when they heard something.

"What is that?" whispered Penelope.

"It sounds like singing," answered Tommy. They all stood still, listening.

"California,
Yes that's the land for me.
I am bound for California
With a washbowl on my knee."

"A prospector," whispered Persifer. "I told you they sing that song."

"Maybe he knows where the mother lode is," Tommy said.

"If he does," Persifer told him, "he surely won't tell us."

Tommy cupped his hands to his mouth. "Hello!" His voice echoed in the canyon.

The singing stopped for a minute, then a voice called back, "Hello!"

The prospector came around a bend in the canyon, leading a mule. The forty-niner was wearing a wide-brimmed hat, a red shirt, and jeans tucked into his boots. The mule was carrying a shovel, a pickax, a large pan, and several sacks. "Hello!" he said. "How's your luck?"

"Not bad," said Penelope. "Hunting for gold?"

"You bet!" said the prospector. "What else would I be doing up here with all these tools?" He waved his hand toward his mule.

"Find any?" asked Persifer.

The prospector looked at them. "Well," he said, "I'll tell you the truth. I heard a man tell a story about a lake high in the mountains that's lined with gold. He said that if you dove into that lake and touched the bottom, you could scoop up gold by the handful. So I came looking for that lake."

"Did you find it?" asked Tommy.

"Nope. I sure didn't. I dipped into every lake I could find up here, until my toes had just about turned blue from the cold, and I didn't find a single lake with a gold bottom."

"That's too bad," said Tommy.

"Yep. Now I know that when a man starts telling a big story about gold, sometimes he's just telling a fairy tale. And once I realized there wasn't any lake of gold, I tried panning along some of the creeks up here, but I never did hit pay dirt. How 'bout you?" asked the prospector. "Have you struck it rich or seen the elephant?"

"Seen the elephant?" asked Susie. "Are there elephants around here too?"

"No," explained Penelope. "'Seen the elephant' means you've been through enough trouble, and you're ready to quit and go home."

"Then we haven't seen the elfelunt!" said Tommy. "We're not gonna quit until we find the mo—"

Persifer grabbed Tommy's arm. "The muddiest stream we can find," he quickly said. "We hear that's where the gold is."

The prospector rubbed his chin. "Hmm, never heard that one before. Well, you're in the wrong place. The streams up here in the mountains all run clear as glass."

Before Tommy could say anything else, Penelope jumped in, saying, "Maybe we'll just look around a little more and then head back down toward the American River."

"With all the forty-niners messing it up, you'll find muddy water down there, that's for sure," he answered. "Well, good luck to you."

"Thanks," said Persifer, "same to you."

"C'mon, Mildred," the prospector said to the mule, "git!" The two headed down the canyon while Tommy and his friends kept going up.

When the babies were out of sight, the prospector stopped and turned around. "Muddy water, my eye," he said to his mule. "They're looking for the mother lode! And they've got a boy with fiery red hair in their company."

The shorty-niners passed through the narrow canyon and reached a waterfall. From high overhead, the water fell into a clear pool, and then tumbled down the mountain. There were large boulders on the sides of the waterfall.

"We'll have to climb," Penelope said. "The map says the mother lode is at the top of this waterfall!"

Helping each other, they all slowly made their way up the rocks. Water from the falls splashed on them.

"The water feels good, huh, Chuckie?" said Tommy.

Chuckie was too worried about slipping off the rocks to enjoy the water. "I guess so, Tommy. But the rocks are kinda slippery."

"Don't worry, Chuckie," Tommy said. "If you fall, you'll just make a great big splash in that pool down there! That'd be fun!" He pulled himself up to the next rock.

"Fun!" said Chuckie. "We don't know what's in that pool! There might be a sea monster!"

"No, Chuckie," Tommy told him, "sea monsters are only in the sea. And that's not the sea.

The sea's a lot bigger than that, I think."

"You're right, Tommy," said Angelica. "There's no sea monster in there. But there's probably a pool monster!"

"Pool monster?" asked Chuckie, his voice shaking a little.

"Yup," answered Angelica, "with big sharp teeth, and a slimy tail, and poker-things coming out of its head!"

"Yaaaah!" yelled Chuckie, scared. He climbed faster to get away from the pool and was the first one to reach the top. He breathlessly stood up, then grinned widely. "Hey," he exclaimed, "I didn't fall!"

"Way to go, Chuckie!" said Tommy.

The others soon joined him. Up on top, the water that made the waterfall was just a small stream coming out of a rock wall. Everywhere they looked, they saw solid rock. There was no tunnel leading into the mother lode.

"Now where do we go, Penelope?" asked Tommy.

"Well," she answered, "let's look at the map again."

"Okay," said Angelica, "but this might be the last time I let you look. I'm tired of holding these two stupid pieces of paper together."

Angelica held up her half, and Penelope studied the map carefully. "The entrance to the mother lode should be right here. The map says there's some kind of cave."

"Maybe it's hidden in the rocks," Persifer said.

"Let's hunt for it," suggested Tommy. They all started searching among the rocks, trying to find an entrance to the cave. They looked and looked, but the rock was smooth everywhere.

After a while, they decided to take a break. Everyone sat on the ground, leaning against a rock wall.

"That map is a fake," said Angelica. "There's no mother lode here at all!"

"Maybe she went somewhere else," suggested Lil.

"Yeah, maybe she went looking for the daddy lode and all her baby lodes," said Phil.

"Or for her grandpa and grandma lode," added Lil. The twins giggled.

"I don't think the map's a fake," Persifer said. "The Miwoks wouldn't trade us a worthless map."

"Yeah, well, it's also said that a redhead would find the mother lode on the mountain," said Angelica. "Did you find anything, Finster?"

"Um," said Chuckie, "I found this flower." He held up a small white flower. It drooped over.

"I think the map comes from a very old trail," Penelope said. "The rocks may have moved since it was drawn."

"Moved?" Angelica scoffed. "How could rocks move? What'd they do—get up and walk?"

Penelope didn't like being laughed at. She frowned. "Of course the rocks didn't walk around. That's not what I meant."

"Then what'd they do?" Angelica asked, laughing. "Skip? Hop? Jump?"

"No, the rocks might have been moved around by an *earthquake*."

Tommy looked confused. "An earth cake?"

"Is it like a mud pie?" asked Lil.

"Mmm," said Phil, rubbing his tummy.

"Not earth cake," Penelope said, "*earthquake.*"

"California has lots of earthquakes," Persifer explained.

"But what's an earthquake?" Tommy asked.

"An earthquake is when the ground—"

But Penelope didn't finish answering Tommy's question because right at that very moment, the ground began to shake. In fact, everything was shaking—the ground, the trees, the water, the rocks . . . and the shorty-niners. It was an earthquake!

Dil laughed. Spike howled. Everyone else yelled and scrambled to get away from falling rocks. Finally, after what seemed like a long time, the shaking stopped.

"That," said Persifer, "was an earthquake."

"Is everybody all right?" asked Penelope. They checked each other, and nobody was hurt. "Thank goodness," said Penelope.

"Hey, where's Chuckie?" Tommy asked.

They looked around. Chuckie had disappeared!

CHAPTER 15

"Chuckie!" Tommy yelled. "Where are you?" They heard something, but it was muffled. Tommy shouted again, "CHUCKIE!"

This time the reply seemed to come from a long way off. "I think it came from over here," said Susie. She ran to the rock wall where Chuckie had been sitting before the earthquake. "Look!" she said.

A crack in the rock had opened up. Now there was a small opening to a narrow tunnel that ran down into the mountain. Tommy toddled over to the opening and stuck his head in the dark hole. "Chuckie!" he yelled again.

A small, scared voice came from inside the tunnel. "Tommy! It's dark in here! Get me out!"

"Don't worry, Chuckie! We're coming!" Tommy turned to Persifer. "Do you have any more rope?"

"No," said Persifer, "I used it all to make the

113

raft. And when the logs broke apart, the rope fell into the stream."

Tommy thought a minute. "That's okay," he said, "I gots another idea. Phil, grab my hand." Phil took Tommy's hand. "Now, Lil, you grab Phil's hand," Tommy said. She did. "Now, everybody grab somebody's hand."

"Are we gonna play a game?" Lil asked Phil.

"Maybe we're gonna play crack-the-whip," Phil answered.

Susie took Lil's other hand, and Persifer took Susie's hand, and Angelica took Persifer's hand, and Penelope took Angelica's hand. Then Penelope held on to Spike's collar. Dil watched from his stroller and clapped his hands.

Tommy led the chain of shorty-niners into the tunnel. The entrance hole was small, but once he slipped inside, Tommy felt around in the dark with his free hand and discovered the tunnel was pretty big. "Chuckie, we're coming!"

"Hurry, it's real scary in here!" cried Chuckie.

Feeling his way carefully along the rock, Tommy made his way down toward Chuckie. "Okay, Chuckie," he said, "take my hand."

"How am I s'posed to do that, Tommy?" Chuckie asked. "I can't see it!"

"Keep talking," said Tommy. "I'll find you."

"What should I talk about? About how the ground started shaking, and all of a sudden I fell backward and rolled and rolled down this dark tunnel until I landed here, and . . . hey!"

Tommy had put his hand right on Chuckie's mouth, guessing where it was by listening. "There you are, Chuckie!" he said.

Chuckie grabbed Tommy's hand. Tommy turned to Susie. "Okay, Susie, let's go back up!" Susie told Phil, and Phil told Lil, and Lil told Persifer . . . all the way up the chain to Penelope, who was standing at the entrance to the tunnel.

"All right, Spike," she said. "Let's go the other way." Spike walked away from the hole in the rock wall, and the shorty-niners came out of the tunnel, with Tommy leading Chuckie at the end.

"We did it!" said Phil and Lil.

"Chuckie, are you okay?" Tommy asked.

"Am I okay? Am I okay?" Chuckie said, upset.

"First I almost get eated by a bear! Then I have to ride a log down a river, and I get all wet! And then I get thrown down a dark, scary tunnel by an earthquake!"

"But, Chuckie! You found the mother lode, just like the legend said you would!" cried Penelope.

"I did?" asked Chuckie.

"Sure! This must be the cave that the map was talking about!"

Hearing that, Angelica dug around in the wagon and found a lantern. Penelope lit the lamp. "Well, what are we waiting for?" Angelica asked. "Let's go and get that gold!"

Everybody went into the tunnel. After they'd gotten out the tools they needed, Persifer hid the wagon by covering it with leaves and branches. He pulled more sticks over the hole in the rock once they were inside. "I don't want anyone to follow us in here," he explained.

"Yeah, like a bear," said Phil.

Chuckie froze. "What if there's already a bear in here?" he asked nervously.

"There won't be, 'cause the door was all

blocked up until the earthquake, remember?" Angelica answered.

For once, Angelica said something that made Chuckie feel better.

"Oh, yeah," he said.

"What if there's another earth cake while we're in here?" asked Lil.

The shorty-niners all looked at each other in the shadowy light of the lamp. They hadn't thought of that.

"There won't be another earthquake," said Angelica bravely. "Let's hurry. C'mon." Carrying the lantern, she started down the tunnel into the cave.

"Why are you leading the way?" Penelope asked.

"'Cause we're all sick of you being in charge, that's why," said Angelica. Actually, she wanted to get to the mother lode first, so she could grab as much gold as possible. "Besides," she added, "I've got the lamp."

"Yes, but it's our lamp," said Persifer.

"Listen to me, buster—" Angelica began, but before she could finish, a cluster of bats flew toward them!

"YAAAAAH!" screamed Chuckie. The others yelled too, surprised by the cloud of flapping black wings.

"It's all right," Susie told them. "My teacher says bats are our friends."

"Bats and snakes," said Angelica, breathing hard. "Your teacher must be a witch."

"If there are bats here—" said Persifer.

Phil frowned. "There are. Lots of 'em."

"Then there must be another way in and out of the cave, even if it's only a little crack big enough for bats." Persifer said, looking worried. "I hope no one else has gotten to the mother lode before us."

The bats flew by. The shorty-niners reached the spot where they'd found Chuckie. From there, the tunnel leveled out, instead of going deeper. Everyone tried to stay close to the lantern, but sometimes they had to feel their way along the rocky walls with their hands.

"Ick!" said Chuckie. "I just touched something yucky."

"What is it?" asked Phil and Lil eagerly.

"I don't know, but it felt slimy."

"Probably a slug," said Persifer.

"Mmm," said Phil, then he called out, "Angelica! I need the lantern to look at a slug, please."

"Stupid babies!" Angelica said. "We're not stopping just so you can eat a yucky slug." She kept walking quickly through the tunnel.

"Sheesh," muttered Phil. "I said 'please.'"

The tunnel kept going. They trudged on in silence for a while, until they heard something—dripping water. The sides of the tunnel felt wet. Drops of water fell from the ceiling. Then they heard a splash!

"Yuck!" said Angelica. "I stepped in some water. Stop, everybody!"

They all stopped at the edge of a pool of water in the tunnel. "It's wet and muddy right here," said Angelica. She set down the lantern and stomped around in the dry part of the tunnel, trying to squish the water out of her shoes.

"Did you hear that, Lil?" said Phil. "It's muddy!"

Lil grinned.

"What are we gonna do?" asked Chuckie. "Maybe there's monsters in that water with poker things coming out of the tops of their heads. . . . Maybe we should just go back."

"We can't go back!" said Tommy. "We gots to find the mother lode!"

"I don't know, Tommy," said Susie, "that water looks pretty—"

But before she could say any more, Phil grabbed the lantern, and he and his sister ran into the muddy water, laughing.

"Wheeee!" Lil said. "It's not deep!"

"But it is good and muddy," Phil said.

Dil laughed and pointed. "Moddy! Moddy!"

Tommy looked at Chuckie, shrugged, and ran after Phil and Lil, kicking water up as he went. The others followed, trying to keep up with the bouncing light.

"Hey! Gimme back that lantern!" yelled Angelica.

They didn't have to go very far before they were soon out of the water. The tunnel started to rise. They climbed up the dark passageway. Then the path got even steeper. Angelica had taken back the lantern, so she walked in front, but she was slowing down.

"I'm getting tired, Tommy," said Chuckie.

"Me too, Chuckie, but we gots to keep going."

They kept following Angelica, staring at the jagged walls and ceiling. Everyone kept hoping to see a glint of gold in the rock. But the stone was dark and dull, with nothing shiny in it except the slimy trails of slugs.

"Why can't we stop somewhere?" asked Phil. "There are lots of slugs here."

"Oh, now you wanna stop," said Angelica. "Before, you just wanted to run right into the yuckiest water in the whole world."

Lil added, "We had to. You were just standing there, talk, talk, talking like growed-ups."

"Well, maybe if you were a little more grown up—" Angelica started to say.

Suddenly Tommy cried out, "Look, guys, a room!"

Just ahead of where Angelica stood, the tunnel opened into a round chamber. Sunlight streamed in through slits in the ceiling high overhead. But there were no other tunnels leading out of the rocky room. This was the end of the cave. And there was no gold.

They followed Angelica as she walked all the way around, holding the lantern high. On one wall they saw smudges of smoke on the rock.

"Look!" said Tommy, pointing.

"What is it?" asked Angelica, excited. "Gold?"

"No," he said, "it's pictures!"

He was right. There were black handprints and red drawings of animals—deer, rabbits, coyotes, wolves, and bears.

"Big deal," said Angelica, "I can draw better than that."

"These drawings look like they've been here for a long, long time," said Persifer. "It's really dusty on the rocks underneath the pictures."

"Maybe somebody came here and took away all the gold," said Susie. "Maybe there's none left!"

"That wouldn't be fair!" said Angelica.

"Maybe these rocks have gold," Lil said.

"No," said Persifer, shaking his head sadly.

"Um, there's no gold here, so let's go look somewhere else," said Chuckie. He'd noticed several bats hanging from the ceiling.

Dil started shaking his rattle, then threw it on the ground. "Rad-o! Rad-o!" he said.

Tommy said, "I'll get it, Dilly." As he picked up the rattle, it scraped away some of the thick dust lying on the floor of the cave. And in the dim light, something gleamed.

Tommy quickly got down on his hands and knees. Brushing away more dust, he found the floor of the cave. It was yellow . . . and shiny! "Angelica," he said, his voice shaking with excitement, "please bring the light over here!"

"What is it?" she asked, walking toward Tommy. "More crummy drawings?"

The light bounced off the yellow patch Tommy had cleared on the floor. "No," he said, "I think it's gold! The whole floor is gold! We're standing right on the mother lode!"

Everyone rushed over to look at the spot Tommy had brushed off. Penelope and Perșifer nodded—it was the mother lode!

CHAPTER 16

Lifting up a pickax, Chuckie grunted. "This is heavy, Tommy." Sweating, Tommy leaned on his shovel and nodded. "I know, Chuckie," he said. "But we're getting lots of gold."

They'd been scraping and digging at the floor for a while now, and they had a pile of gold chunks. It glowed in the light of the lantern.

"How much gold do you think we need?" Chuckie asked Tommy.

"Well," Tommy said, "I don't know if we can ever find this place again, so we'd better get enough to last a long time." Nodding, Chuckie hit the floor with the pickax. Then Tommy used his shovel to loosen the pieces of gold.

Angelica was digging as fast as she could, dreaming of all the Cynthia accessories she'd have—the Cynthia Scuba-Diving Set, the Cynthia Ski Lodge, the Cynthia Airport . . .

Phil and Lil kept digging, hoping they'd find some worms too.

"This is wonderful!" said Persifer as he dug into the floor, "a real bonanza!"

Spike was helping to dig too. After Susie used a pickax to break up the floor, Spike dug out the gold with his paws.

Even Dil was helping. Tommy gave him a little hammer and set him down on the floor. Dil started banging away at the gold, helping to break it up.

Persifer checked the lantern. "There's not much kerosene left. We've got to head out."

They took the gold they'd dug out of the floor and put it in sacks, pans, Angelica's backpack, and even in Dil's stroller.

Chuckie tried to pick up one of the sacks of gold. "Umph! This is really heavy."

Tommy agreed that the gold weighed a lot. "I don't think we can carry more gold back down the mountain."

"I'm not even sure we can carry all this," said Susie.

They loaded up as much of the gold as they

could carry, and headed back out the long, dark tunnel.

When they finally pushed aside the branches hiding the entrance and stepped back outside, it was dark. The sky was full of stars.

The babies were so tired, they were almost falling asleep standing up. "I'm so tired, I could fall asleep even if the Dummi Bears were on TB," said Phil. The others nodded.

"I'm so tired, I could fall asleep even if Reptar was standing right here," said Tommy.

"I'm so tired," said Chuckie, "I could . . . zzzzzzz." He curled up on the ground.

"Before we all fall asleep," Persifer said, "we have to hide this gold." He pulled Chuckie to his feet.

Angelica patted her backpack. "I'm keeping my gold right with me. I can use it as a pillow."

"No," said Persifer. "We have to hide it somewhere better than that. Like in this hollow tree." He patted the trunk of an old tree near the mouth of the tunnel.

"Okay," said Tommy sleepily. The others agreed.

They took the bags and pans of gold and emptied them into a hole in the trunk of the tree.

"There," said Penelope, "that's better. Now we can go to sleep."

It was chilly. They covered themselves with blankets and lay down next to the biggest rocks, trying to stay out of the wind. The ground wasn't comfortable, but they were exhausted, and the sound of the waterfall below them was as soothing as a lullaby, so they soon fell fast asleep.

Chuckie snuck into a cave. On the other side of the cave was a big gold throne. He started picking up hunks of gold and putting them in a sack. He put in more and more, until the sack was bigger than he was. Then he grabbed the mouth of the sack, gave it a twist, and lifted the whole thing onto his back. Gee, he thought, I'm stronger than I thought I was.

But just as he started to leave the room, a door in the rock swung open. A shiny gold man wearing a gold crown walked in. "Ah," he said, "time to sit on my gold throne. I love to . . . hey, what are you doing?" He was staring right at Chuckie.

The Gold Man! thought Chuckie. I've got to get out of here! He started to run.

"Stop, thief!" yelled the Gold Man, chasing after Chuckie.

But the bag on Chuckie's back was heavy, and he ran more and more slowly. The Gold Man soon caught up with him. "Trying to steal my gold, are you?" he shouted as he clamped a cold metal hand on Chuckie's shoulder.

"YAAAAAAAAAAH!!!!!" Chuckie screamed.

Chuckie sat straight up. It was still night, but the moon had risen and was shining brightly on the rocks. "A dream," he said to himself, "it was just a dream. Well, a nightmare."

He rubbed his eyes and looked around. Everyone was sleeping. Then he saw someone over by the hollow tree! Whoever it was noticed Chuckie looking at him and walked over quickly.

It was Persifer. "Chuckie," he said, "a noise woke me up. Did you hear anything?"

"No," Chuckie answered.

"All right. Go back to sleep," said Persifer.

In the morning the shorty-niners woke up to a beautiful day. The sun was shining, the wind had died down, and the birds were singing. Tommy stretched and smiled. He thought about all the Reptar Bars they'd be able to get. He walked over to the hollow tree and peeked inside.

The gold was gone!

"Oh, no!" cried Tommy. "The gold!"

"What about it?" asked Angelica, rubbing her eyes.

"It's gone!"

"Gone?"

Everyone rushed over to the tree. One by one they stuck their heads in the hole and looked into the trunk. There wasn't a single piece of gold.

"It's been stolen!" said Persifer.

"Well, duh," said Angelica. "It didn't grow wings and fly away."

"Who took it?" asked Phil.

"I know who took it," said Lil.

"Who?" they all asked eagerly.

"A thief."

"Of course it was a thief, you stupid baby!" said Angelica.

Chuckie remembered something. "Hey, Persifer heard something."

"How do you know?" asked Angelica.

"He told me. I had a nightmare, so I woked up and I saw Persifer by the tree, and he told me he heard something."

Angelica turned to Persifer. "So you were by the tree?" she asked suspiciously.

"Yes," he said. "I heard a noise, so I got up to check the gold."

"Was it still there?" asked Susie.

"Of course," Persifer said. "If it had been gone, I would have gotten all of you up."

"What kinda noise did you hear, Persifer?" asked Tommy.

"A sort of scratching sound," Persifer said.

"Did you see anybody around the tree?" Tommy asked.

"No," said Persifer.

"Maybe you didn't see anybody," Angelica

said, "because you stole the gold yourself!"

Everyone gasped.

"That's ridiculous!" said Persifer.

"Oh, yeah?" said Angelica. "You got up in the night to steal the gold, but Chuckie woke up and saw you, so you told him you heard a noise. After he went back to sleep, you took the gold."

"Why'd you do it, Persifer?" asked Lil.

"I didn't!" he said. He turned his pockets inside out. "See? Nothing!"

"You stole my map," Angelica said, "so we already know you're a thief. Where's the gold?"

"I took that map so I could give it back to my sister. I am not a thief!" Persifer turned to Penelope. "Tell them, Penelope! Tell them I'm not a thief!"

Penelope looked at her brother. Then she spoke to Angelica. "If you think my brother took the gold, why don't you search through his things to see if he's got it hidden?"

"That's ezzackly what I plan to do," said Angelica. She starting looking through the wagon and all the bundles of clothes and equipment, hunting for the missing gold.

131

Tommy whispered to Chuckie, "I don't think Persifer stole the gold, Chuckie."

"Why not, Tommy?" asked Chuckie.

"'Cause he's been nice to us, and helped us."

"Then who took the gold?"

"I don't know, but I'm gonna find out."

Angelica searched through everything, but she didn't find the gold.

"See?" said Persifer. "I didn't take it."

"Maybe you hid it somewhere around here," said Angelica. "Then you were going to come back and get it later."

"And maybe," said Persifer, "you took it! Maybe you're just saying it's me because you're the one who's guilty!"

"Why'd you do it, Angelica?" asked Lil.

"I didn't!" she yelled.

"Well, somebody took the gold," said Phil.

Just then they heard singing.

"California,
Yes that's the land for me.
I am bound for California
With a washbowl on my knee."

"It's that prospector!" said Susie.

The singing stopped, but they could hear pots and pans clanking as they bounced against the prospector's mule. The shorty-niners went to the edge of the big rocks at the top of the waterfall and looked down. The prospector was standing beside the pool with his mule. He looked up and saw the babies. "All right if I come up?" called the prospector.

"Um, sure!" said Susie. The prospector tied his mule to a tree and started climbing. Susie turned to the others. "Maybe he can help figure out where our gold went."

"Or maybe," Angelica said, thinking hard, "he stole our gold himself!"

"Then why would he come back here?" asked Persifer.

"To throw us off the penny!" said Angelica.

"You mean throw us off the scent," corrected Susie.

"I hope he doesn't throw us off these rocks," said Phil.

The prospector soon reached the top of the waterfall. "How'd that muddy water work out for you? Find any?"

"Yeah," said Phil, "in the cave." Angelica punched him in the arm. "Ow!" said Phil.

"What cave?" asked the prospector eagerly.

"Oh," said Persifer casually, "just a little cave we saw on the way here." He glanced at the entrance to the cave, making sure they'd hidden it well with sticks, rocks, and leaves. "Phil loves caves," he added.

"I do?" Phil asked. "Yeah, I do!"

"Well," said the prospector, "if you're going to go poking around in caves, make sure you've got all the right equipment—lamps, rope, hobnailed boots . . ."

"What are hop-tailed boots?" asked Tommy.

"*Hob*nailed boots." The prospector lifted up his feet proudly. "Like these. See the hobnails in the soles?"

Tommy saw the little nails on the bottoms of his shoes. He nodded.

"Keeps you from slipping, even on wet rock," the prospector said.

"Okay, Mr. Prospector," said Angelica, "enough talking. What did you do with our gold?"

Tommy wandered back to the hollow tree.

"What?" asked the prospector, startled. "What in tarnation are you talking about?"

"The gold, that's what I'm talking about," said Angelica. "The gold you stole from us last night."

"Didn't even know you had any gold! Where'd you find it?"

"I'm asking the questions here," said Angelica. "Where'd you put our gold after you sneaked it out of the tree?"

Tommy was looking around the hollow tree. He looked up into its branches.

"You found gold in a tree?" said the prospector. "That's a new one on me. Never heard of gold growing on trees."

"WHERE IS OUR GOLD?" Angelica yelled.

"Now, settle down there, missy," he said. "I'll admit I came up here hoping to find the mother lode. I figured that was what you were looking for, and now it sounds like maybe you found it. I've been hunting for gold an awfully long time now, and I haven't had much luck. I thought maybe you'd change that, especially with that fire-haired boy around. But I didn't steal your gold. I'm not a thief."

Susie and Penelope nodded at each other. The prospector sounded honest.

"If you're not a thief," said Angelica, "then you won't mind if we search through the bags on your mule."

"Nope," said the prospector, "I wouldn't mind a bit. You go right ahead."

"Fine," said Angelica stubbornly, "I will." She started to climb down the rocks by the waterfall to the mule. The others were about to follow, when Tommy cried, "Stop, Angelica!"

"What is it, Tommy?" she asked, annoyed. "I'm kinda busy catching a robber."

"You don't have to climb down those rocks."

"Why not?"

"Because I know who took the gold!"

CHAPTER 17

"You do?" asked Chuckie.

"Yup," said Tommy, "I figured it out."

"Tell us, Tommy!" said Susie.

"Who took the gold?" asked Penelope. "Where is it?"

Tommy walked over to the prospector, who was sitting on a rock, and said, "Please stand up."

The prospector looked mad. "I'm telling you, I didn't steal your gold!"

"I know you didn't," said Tommy. "I just want to show 'em you didn't."

The prospector stood up. "Walk a bit," said Tommy. He took three steps.

"Look, everybody," said Tommy. They all gathered around. "See his feetsprints? Those nails in his boots make funny marks in the dirt." Everyone nodded. They could see the marks.

Then Tommy led them to the hollow tree. "I looked all around the tree, but I didn't find any feetsprints with funny marks like that."

"So?" said Angelica.

"So he didn't walk around here. How could he take the gold out if he didn't walk over to the tree?"

"Um," said Phil, "he used a shovel with a real long handle?"

"No," said Tommy, "he didn't take the gold."

"So it was Persifer!" cried Angelica. "I knew it!"

"No, it wasn't Persifer," said Tommy.

"That's right!" said Persifer.

"He got all the gold he could carry yesterday," said Tommy. "Why would he steal all of ours, too?"

"Because he's greedy!" yelled Angelica.

"No, he isn't, Angelica," said Tommy. "He didn't take the gold."

"Then who stole the gold?" asked Susie.

Tommy leaned against the tree. "Persifer said he heard a scratching sound. Sometimes I hear scratching sounds in the trees in our backyard. You know who makes those?"

"Spike?" guessed Lil.

"Well, sometimes," said Tommy. "Then I

looked at the tree again. But this time I didn't look down, I looked up."

He looked up, and so did the others. High in the tree, they saw a clump of sticks and leaves. And then they saw something yellow flash in the sun!

"The gold!" cried Persifer.

"In a squirrel's nest!" said Susie.

"Right!" said Tommy. "The scratching noise Persifer heard was squirrels! They stole our gold!"

Chuckie laughed. "They probably thought the lumps of gold were nuts!"

"You found lumps of gold?" the prospector asked, amazed.

"But how could all our gold fit in one lousy nest?" Angelica asked.

"It didn't," Tommy said. "Look!"

He pointed to the other trees around them. They all had squirrels' nests, and in each of the nests, gold could be seen shining.

"Well, I'll be doggoned," said the prospector. "Gold does grow on trees."

CHAPTER 18

With Spike chasing the squirrels away, the shorty-niners boosted each other up into the trees to gather the gold. Even the prospector helped.

"Here," said Tommy, holding out a bag to the prospector, "you can have this gold. Thanks for helping us."

"You're welcome, Tommy," said the prospector. He opened the bag and peeked inside. "Whaa-hoo!" he yelled. "Eureka!"

"Persifer?" said Angelica.

"Yes, Angelica?" he said.

"I'm sorry I called you a thief. I guess you and your sister helped us a lot."

"Thanks," he said.

"Even if she is awfully bossy," Angelica whispered.

After they had gotten all the gold, the shorty-niners prepared to climb down the waterfall and start the long walk back.

Suddenly the ground began to shake again!

"Another earthquake!" yelled Persifer.

The trees shook. Rocks fell from the mountain above them.

Then the shaking stopped.

Tommy looked over at the entrance to the cave. Huge rocks had fallen in front of it, covering it up. He smiled, knowing the mother lode was hidden again.

"Oh, no!" said Lil.

"What's the matter?" asked Phil.

"I dropped my bag, and all the gold lumps spilled out!"

"Don't worry, Lil," said Tommy, "we'll help you find them."

"I think they rolled under these bushes."

Tommy, Chuckie, Phil, Lil, Susie, Angelica, and even Dil crawled under the bushes to find the lumps of gold. Sniffing along the ground, Spike followed them.

Tommy crawled out from the bush. He saw a sandbox, a ball, a patio—he was back in his own yard! "Guys," he said, "that was one of our bestest adventures ever!"

Susie nodded. "It was also one of our longest adventures."

"Yeah," said Angelica, "I've had 'bout enough of you stupid babies." She struggled to pull off her heavy backpack. "I'm gonna go look at the Cynthia catalog and pick out what I want . . . like the Cynthia Snowboard and the Cynthia Jet Plane and the Cynthia Ice-Cream Shop . . ." Still talking, she went into the house.

"Susie!"

"That's my mom calling. I gotta go."

"Bye!" said Tommy. "See you tomorrow!"

Tommy turned to Chuckie, who was still crawling out from under the bushes. "Come on, Chuckie," said Tommy. "Let's go get those Reptar Bars!"

"Yay!" shouted Phil and Lil. "Reptar Bars!"

"But, Tommy," Chuckie said, "don't we have to go to the store to get Reptar Bars?"

Tommy thought for a minute. Then he smiled. "I know!" he said. "We'll show all our gold to my mommy, and then she'll know that we wanna go to the store."

The four of them ran through the back door into the kitchen. Didi and Betty were lying on the floor with their heads under the sink.

"There!" said Betty. "That oughta hold it!"

"I certainly hope so," said Didi. "The mop's just about worn out!"

Didi sat up and saw Tommy, Chuckie, Phil, and Lil holding out their hands.

"My, you pups have been busy," Betty said as she got up. "That's a lot of rocks and pebbles you have there."

"Oh, Tommy," said Didi, "look how dirty you got! We're going to have to give you all a bath!"

"Yeah," agreed Betty, "but they sure did play together for a nice, long time. These pups deserve a reward." She dug around in her tool belt and pulled out . . . four Reptar Bars! "There you go," Betty said, passing out the chocolate bars. The babies grinned, and they each handed her a pebble.

"Aw, you don't have to pay me," she said with a chuckle, "but I'll take 'em, if you insist. These rocks are as good as gold!"

About the Author

David Lewman has written many books featuring the Rugrats, including *The Rugrats' Joke Book*, *More Jokes!*, books in the Rugrats "A Day in the Life" series, and *A Rugrats Night Before Christmas*. He also wrote the dialogue and lyrics for a musical, *Adventures with Young King Arthur*. As a writer for *Nickelodeon Magazine*, David has penned over one hundred articles and humor pieces, and will travel far and wide to get a story done. Once he even went on a plane dressed as a garment bag! David lives in California and used to collect rocks, but is sorry to say that he's never found any gold.